M000214612

Dear Reader,

In the opening story of *Th[e ...]* slices a mango. This seen[...] autopsy—an unnerving a[...] [...] esque precision and control. With the careful carving of a blade, a stunning exploration of migration, loss, and Central American identity unfolds.

When I first read this story, I was captivated. It was strange but elegant, terrifying but beautiful. So were the stories that followed. Ruben Reyes Jr. is a natural storyteller; his stories are meticulously architectured, sharp with political, social, and emotional specificity. An ordinary man transforms into a Latin pop star. An aging abuela morphs into a marionette. A son desperate to save his family is thrown into a detention center on Mars. The last story subverts the choose-your-own-storyline trope, catapulting the reader into one boy's harrowing migration journey, where reverberations of a single choice could mean triumph or tragedy, life or death. With influences ranging from Franz Kafka to George Saunders to Selena Quintanilla to Camila Cabello, Ruben's work is breathtaking in its scope, unlimited in its approach.

This collection will delight you, haunt you, invigorate you, and make you think. It calls to mind Anthony Veasna So's *Afterparties* and Nana Kwame Adjei-Brenyah's *Friday Black* as well as shows like *Black Mirror* and *Severance*. We are taken to far-off worlds only to stumble on the same questions that plague our own. What is the cost of migration? How do you exist in a world you were forced into? What does it mean to wake up one day and realize your life no longer belongs to you? With humor, insight, and heart, Ruben finds answers. Those answers always make our world seem more hopeful and stranger—or more hopeful because it is stranger. Out of this strangeness, possibilities for a kinder world grow.

I'm thrilled to share Ruben's collection with you.

JESSICA VESTUTO
ASSOCIATE EDITOR
MARINER BOOKS

THERE IS A RIO GRANDE IN HEAVEN

THERE IS A
RIO GRANDE
IN HEAVEN

STORIES

RUBEN REYES JR.

MARINER BOOKS   *New York   Boston*

THERE IS A RIO GRANDE IN HEAVEN. Copyright © 2024 by Ruben Reyes Jr. All rights reserved. Printed in the United States of America. No part of this book may be used or reproduced in any manner whatsoever without written permission except in the case of brief quotations embodied in critical articles and reviews. For information, address HarperCollins Publishers, 195 Broadway, New York, NY 10007.

HarperCollins books may be purchased for educational, business, or sales promotional use. For information, please email the Special Markets Department at SPsales@harpercollins.com.

FIRST EDITION

Interior art by Marina Demidova

Designed by Chloe Foster

Library of Congress Cataloging-in-Publication Data has been applied for.

ISBN 978-0-06-333627-8

23 24 25 26 27 LBC 5 4 3 2 1

In memory of Juan Cañadas

País mío no existes
sólo eres una mala silueta mía
una palabra que le creí al enemigo

ROQUE DALTON, "EL GRAN DESPECHO"

I was in love, then, with monsters and skeletons and
circuses and carnivals and dinosaurs and, at last, the
red planet, Mars.

RAY BRADBURY, *ZEN IN THE ART OF WRITING*

CONTENTS

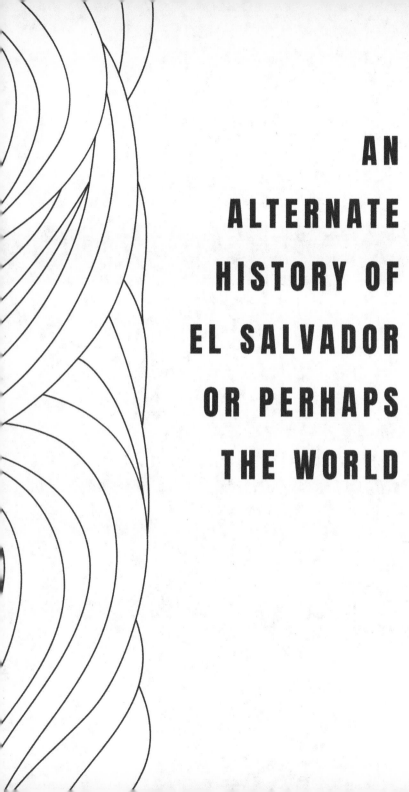

AN
ALTERNATE
HISTORY OF
EL SALVADOR
OR PERHAPS
THE WORLD

THE SPANISH SHIPS LEAVE THEIR DOCKS, but there is no crash landing, no savior knocking at the isthmus's shore—only civilization as it was and continues to be. A tempest thrashes *La Niña* around as men fall off her side in a choir of shrieks and prayers. An empire-size wave swells and crashes down on *La Pinta*, splintering the cork-oak frame and pine planks. The *Santa Maria* sinks, full of salty-sweet water, until it sits on the ocean floor. Bottom-feeders nibble on dead Spaniards' skin.

Another attempt, decades later. This is how the story goes: Thousands of Pipil stand before the Spanish soldiers with spears in their hands, obsidian blades pointed toward the rain clouds as they prepare for a battle that will determine who stays and who leaves this land they know as Cuscatlán, or San Salvador; one name Spanish, one name true. The Spanish are on horses, the Pipil on foot, and the air soon fills with the sound of gunfire and screams, the battlefield soaked in gunpowder and horse blood.

The Pipil soldiers find themselves on the precipice of defeat. Enslavement is almost guaranteed. Their skin branded with a red-hot iron, their bodies shipped to a land other than this. They fight, though their cotton-armor is soaked and heavy. Outmanned, losing men by the second, they continue swinging and jabbing. Mud makes their dark skin darker.

Then the clouds shift. The rain intensifies, each droplet expanding into a heavy orb. In the deluge, a Pipil soldier sees an opening and lunges forward. The Spanish army commander's hair sticks to his forehead as he falls from his horse, pierced in the side by a spear tip. He tumbles into the quagmire, and his blood mixes with brown water. If he doesn't die there, an infection will inevitably kill him.

The Pipil win the battle, and the Spanish never return. 1524 marks a continuation. The year signifies neither murderous start nor massacred end.

Onward, forevermore. The coast is quiet. Death is just a part of the rainforest's life cycle, a cosmic part of Earth's give-and-take. There is no war, no aftermath, no nation. No blood or sweat or singed skin in the dirt.

HE
EATS
HIS
OWN

EVERY MORNING, AT 8:05 A.M., NETO PULLED out his white plastic cutting board and placed one fresh mango on it. As if conducting an autopsy, he placed the tip of the knife at the top and made a slow, deliberate incision down to the base of the fruit. He repeated the action five times, cutting around the seed until he ended up with six perfect slices. Neto picked each one up by the skin, careful to avoid touching the soft yellow flesh, and placed it into a bowl he'd pulled from above the counter.

Then he washed the cutting board in the sink, dried it with a freshly pressed dishrag, and put it away, out of sight. Neto's kitchen was spotless, everything hidden in the cabinets above the marble counter. It was the opposite of the clutter his parents kept at their home when he was growing up, the kind that accumulates when ghosts from the third world prevent you from throwing anything away.

Around 4:30 P.M., Tomas climbed down from Neto's mango tree slowly, careful not to disturb a single leaf. He'd broken a branch once, sending three mangoes toppling to the ground, and had received a beating that had left him sore and with a scar that never quite went away. Tomas clutched the day's harvest close to his chest, secured the padlock on the corrugated metal fence protecting the tree, and ran down the trail leading back to his home.

The brick-wall, dirt-floor home his family lived in had two dining tables. The first was a rectangular table with chipped black paint. This is where they ate dinner. The second was mahogany, covered with a plastic sheet that was easy to disinfect. This was where the mangoes went.

Tomas's tiny hands held the bag wide open for his mother. Round and round she turned each mango, inspecting every bit of its reddish orange skin. If the mango was imperfect, she'd throw it into the red basket at the foot of the table, her frustration growing with each toss. They needed ten impeccable mangoes. Tomas's favorites were the mangoes with wormholes because Mami would cut out the ugly bits and let him eat the rest. At high season, he'd sneak fresh ones, even though his parents and cousin forbade it. No one would find the pit in the brush that lined the path to the mango tree.

That afternoon, Tomas brought home a perfect batch; no worms, bruises, or unwanted holes left by hungry birds. Each mango was firm but would be perfectly ripe when they arrived at their destination. Delicately, as if handling diamonds, Mami took each mango and put it in the crate. A cushion padded the bottom, and the sides were lined with felt. She packed the mangoes close together, placing folded rags between them to ensure they wouldn't shift in transit.

At 10:30 P.M., Papi carried the crate into the passenger seat of his 2001 Toyota Camry, as he did every night. His shoulders, carefully shaped by hours of farmwork, peeked out from his thin white tank top. Tomas watched his muscles flex and relax like the bubbling creek he crossed on the way to Neto's mango tree. Papi turned on the ignition and made the seventy-five-minute drive from Guazapa to the airport.

Instead of pulling up to the front of the terminals, where family members kissed travelers bearing cardboard boxes full of cheap clothing, Papi went to the back of the airport. In a year and a half of deliveries, he'd never brought a box with a missing or stowaway fruit. A flight attendant counted them anyway, though he profusely apologized. He didn't doubt that Papi was a trustworthy man, but he had orders to follow.

Papi signed a contract saying he'd delivered the fruit and, shortly after, the ten mangoes were placed onto a wheelchair and pushed into the airport. By the time Papi had returned to his little home in Guazapa, the mangoes were strapped into an economy seat on a five-hour flight to Los Angeles International Airport. Neto always bought all three seats in a row, so the mangoes could travel undisturbed.

Neto's boyfriend hated mangoes. It hadn't always been that way, but after so many mango smoothies, meats served with a mango reduction sauce, and unevenly chopped pieces of mango in his salads, the mere sight of the fruit angered Steven. Once, at the Whole Foods that had replaced a shop specializing in Central American imports, he purposefully knocked over a stack of boxed mangoes. It was all caught on camera and the manager forced him to pay for everything under the threat of arrest, which made Steven despise mangoes even more.

He would never tell Neto how deeply his hatred went. When he admitted he was getting sick of mangoes, Neto had been incredibly understanding, cutting back on the flavor whenever he cooked for them. But still, the fruit's mere presence bothered Steven, so much so that he changed his work schedule to leave their apartment before Neto got back from the airport. He couldn't stand the sight of Neto cutting up his breakfast.

Still, he loved Neto for many reasons. Neto was generous with his time and attention, a generosity he extended to Steven and his own parents in equal measure. They'd met a decade earlier, before either of them lived in Los Angeles, at one of those fancy northeastern universities where tuition was higher than the national median income. Neto came from modest money and Steven from nearly none, which meant that they didn't run in the same circles: different parties, different extra-curriculars, different friends. On their fifth date, they realized they'd attended the same *Scarface*-themed party as sophomores. It was the only social event they remembered being at together. "Impossible to believe I missed a face as handsome as yours in that crowd," Neto had said.

They reconnected at a crummy alumni reunion put on in Orange County, organized by folks who had graduated at a time when racial slurs were still en vogue and an interracial gay re-lationship raised major eyebrows. As two of the youngest men there, and by far the handsomest, they slowly drifted to each other. When Neto very vaguely mentioned working in finance, Steven's interest deflated, but then he made a quip about being as well endowed as the university, and that was enough reason for Steven feel him out a bit longer. The handsome and rich so seldom needed a personality.

A real attraction emerged from the elitist petri dish of a hotel ballroom and Neto fed it. He made time for dates with Steven, despite working arduous hours and unexpected overtime. He paid for day trips and overnight stays in Joshua Tree and Big Bear. Steven was merely smitten at first, but then fell fully in love with a man who looked at him as if there were nothing more precious in the world. When Neto asked him to move in, Steven didn't flinch.

They'd been living together for about three months when Neto finally told Steven about his mango tree. Steven laughed at first, but by the end of the night he'd left the apartment, feign-ing a trip to the gym. Instead, he went to Yogurtland and filled a medium-size cup. Steven surveyed the toppings, calculating whether the kiwi chunks would be lighter than the strawberry slices, and therefore cheaper, until the sight of syrupy, con-gealed mango bits put him off fruit entirely. He ate plain vanilla in silence, trying to make sense of what Neto had told him.

Neto's morning drive to LAX was perfect for organizing the loose ends of his life. He called his mother, who was recently on his ass for not keeping in touch.

"It's been three weeks since I've seen you," she said. Her filtered voice rushed out of the car speakers. She still lived in Neto's childhood home, on a suburban street full of empty nesters. He visited as often as his work schedule allowed, but it never felt like enough, so he called her almost daily to keep her at bay. The past couple of weeks, though, the strategy was only moderately successful. "Three weeks. I've been counting."

"They're selling units in a new apartment building in the Arts District, not too far from my place," Neto said. "I can buy you and Papi one. It'd be easier to see each other if you didn't live all the way out in Diamond Bar."

She tsk-tsked and said it'd be too small. They rehashed the same conversation every couple of months. Neto was willing to buy his parents an apartment, so long as they downsized. The boxes of Christmas decorations, the extra sets of kitchenware, the bags of old hand-me-downs his mother insisted she'd eventually take to his relatives in El Salvador—all of it had to go. Neto told them to leave everything behind, and that he'd furnish the apartment with entirely new things. But his mother hated hearing that, insisting that she needed every piece of her hundred-piece nativity scene. Every box of trinkets was a treasure chest.

"Have you talked to your tia recently?" she asked, changing the subject. The boxes of mangoes arrived fine, so Neto hadn't.

"Send her a little extra this week," she said. "She woke up with a massive headache this morning. She won't ask for it, but she needs money to pay for a doctor's visit and whatever they might prescribe."

Neto was pulling up into the airport parking lot, so he promised he would and hung up. When he'd first conceived of the scheme, a deliveryman handled the pickup, but a few weeks in, an aching anxiety set in. Neto spent the earliest hours of his day, which used to be his most productive, worrying. His mangoes were so sweet, so delicious, and he relied on them the way Steven relied on his antidepressants. The delivery took on an almost mythic quality. If he didn't get his mangoes, everything else he'd built for himself would fall apart too. Until the doorbell rang, Neto was useless, so he began making the drive himself.

Travelers emerged from a hallway below the waiting area. As they climbed up the ramp, pushing carts full of luggage, their loved ones tried desperately to spot them. By now Neto had cataloged the kinds of hugs exchanged at the airport, hinging on three factors: relationship between the embracers, time gone without having seen each other, and gender of the involved parties. A mother who was reuniting with her son after his two-month summer trip in El Salvador would give a tight embrace, but she wouldn't cry. She'd be smiling nonstop. A hug from a daughter who hadn't seen her father for more than a decade— because either the visa or money wasn't there—would be different. She'd embrace him tightly, like the mother reuniting with her son, but she'd loosen her grip much sooner, realizing that her papi was frailer, wrinklier. Both would cry. Change the daughter into a son, and only the father would let out a few well-controlled tears. Most reunions, though bittersweet, were joyous, brimming with the sort of elation Neto felt seeing Steven after a business trip.

Neto stood alone, waiting, quietly taking in the tears, embraces, laughter, and aroma of Pollo Campero that filled the terminal. When he caught sight of the flight attendant around the corner, pushing a wheelchair with a box of mangoes strapped in, he finally let his guard down. The sight softened his heart, opening it to the other airport-goers' fervor. Relief and joy rushed him. If he could perform this man-made miracle, again and again, nothing would get in his way.

He handed the flight attendant a ten-dollar tip, hugged the box close to his chest, and made the drive home. By the time he pulled out his cutting board, he'd forgotten about sending the extra money for his aunt.

The night of Neto's confession, before he had gotten sick of the mangoes, Steven scraped the bottom of his cup with his spoon and laid out what he'd been told.

Neto owned a mango tree in El Salvador. He'd planted it a few years ago, while he was on a trip with his parents. It was on a plot of land that belonged to his uncle. Three summers later, he returned and finally tasted one of the mangoes. They were the best mangoes he'd ever eaten. Neto smuggled a few into the United States, sliced up and hidden in a box of chocolates at the bottom of his luggage. He tried to forget about his tree for a few years, though his mouth watered for its fruit. Once he'd been made general partner at his firm, he realized that he could have the bliss he sought. He called his aunt, uncle, and cousin in Guazapa and told them his plan. He wanted them to pick mangoes daily, ensure they were the best ones on the tree at the time, and have them shipped to him on a commercial flight. It was a favor for a family member, Neto argued. And he'd give them extra cash to help cover some living expenses. They wouldn't have to bow to the whims of the season's harvest, like other families in their cantón.

Steven repeated the facts to himself. Neto owned a mango tree in El Salvador. He spent exorbitant amounts of money daily so he could taste its fruit from two thousand miles away.

When the mangoes stopped coming, Neto couldn't complain. The circumstances were too tragic.

His uncle had been caught in those rogue bouts of violence that plagued so much of their bite-size country. On one of his trips to the airport, a group of men blocked the highway and stopped him. They forced him to step out of the car and roughed him around a bit before taking his cell phone and all the cash he carried with him. The box of mangoes was in the passenger seat, but the mareros ignored the precious cargo. Then they told Neto's uncle he'd be welcome to use the road anytime he wanted, as long as he paid a toll. Shaking, but alive, he continued to the airport.

Over the course of the next month, he was stopped three more times, his anger festering with every extortion payment. On the fourth stop, he refused to hand over the five measly bills. The consequences made it into the folds of *La Prensa Gráfica*: fifty-year-old man found in his Camry, on the side of Autopista Comalapa, with a bullet hole in his head.

Neto wanted to go to the funeral, but it was the firm's busiest season. He couldn't get the time off. He watched a live stream of the procession. His uncle had been a tall man, but because no one around town had a minivan to lend for his procession, Mami and Tomas settled for a midsize SUV. The end of Papi's coffin stuck out from the back of the car as the crowd of mourners followed it around the town's narrow streets. Tomas and Mami trailed the makeshift hearse, followed closely by the priest and two musicians strumming and singing hymns. For the first time in a long time, they'd forgotten about Neto's mangoes.

Neto had not. It'd been three weeks since his last shipment, and his life was already splintering. He was arguing with Steven more often. His bosses were riding his ass. Nothing tasted as delicious as his mangoes. He ate a spoonful of cereal, and the milk was sour. He tried three different grocery stores—Whole Foods,

Erewhon, Sprouts—but no one's produce compared. Nights became longer as he lay awake worrying that he'd never taste them again. If the mangoes rotted at the base of his tree in Guazapa, Neto's carefully constructed life would disintegrate too.

Neto called to ask how he was doing, so Tomas told the truth. Without his father, he felt less safe. The cantón was lousy with dangers that certainly had existed before, but that Papi had shielded him from: drunks with machetes, thieves without morals, dark sleepless nights.

"I'm really sorry," Neto said. "Would a distraction help?"

At his cousin's suggestion, Tomas taught Mami to drive in a used pickup truck, one Neto paid for. Papi had taught him the basics, and after a few lessons Mami was confident enough to drive on the highway. Hopeful that the mareros wouldn't harm a woman, and needing the money, Mami began delivering the mangoes to the airport.

Two months. That's how long Papi had been six feet under with the bones of guerrilleros and government soldiers before misery found shelter in Tomas's home again, as if it were a lost dog, one of those aguacateros that roam rural Salvadoran villages. Mami fell while she was putting tortillas onto the comal in the kitchen. Fifteen minute later, once she had managed to sit up but still struggled to stand, Tomas leaned her against his small frame and walked her to the doctor.

Mami said it was heartbreak. The doctor said it was a coronary disease that would only worsen without surgery. The procedure would be expensive, and Mami didn't trust the doctors in their rural slice of the country. She was trying to figure out a way of affording a surgeon in San Salvador when Tomas overheard her on the phone with her sister. Tomas never talked to his aunt, Neto's mother, but he could tell the woman was trying to convince Mami to come to the United States. The doctors were better in Los Angeles. Neto could help them apply for a visa. Mami was hesitant, but by the time she hung up the phone, she'd agreed to try what her sister suggested.

"I don't want to leave Papi here," Tomas said.

"We carry him here," Mami said, pressing a palm to her chest. "Always."

Steven and Neto had only argued about the mango tree once. Steven had let his real feelings slip. It was an irresponsible use of money, especially when there were struggling nonprofits and underfunded community centers throughout the city.

"It's hard to see you waste money like this. I know what it's like to go without," Steven said.

"And I don't," Neto conceded. "But my parents didn't spoil me growing up. The mangoes are a luxury. It's also a way of helping my family. Both things can be true."

Neto didn't want to reopen the argument, so he told half the truth: He was bringing his aunt to the United States for a surgery. Neto knew how important his aunt's calls were to his mother. She was her last connection to El Salvador, so Neto would do what he could to help. He cared for her too. If helping his aunt meant she'd be healthy enough to return to Guazapa, where she could tend to the mango tree again, that was a welcome bonus. The mangoes had *just* returned, reintroducing stability into his life.

Together, he and Steven researched requirements and helped his aunt fill out an application for a B-2 visa. Neto paid the fees and sent the embassy bank statements that proved he'd be able to cover the medical costs himself. The doctor had told his aunt that she had a bit of time, but that she shouldn't wait too long before undergoing surgery. Every day that passed without a response from the embassy sent a wave of anxiety through the family. Tomas might lose his mother. Neto's mother could lose her sister. A fresh mango greeted Neto each morning, but he worried it'd be his last.

When the visa applications were denied, Neto appealed and funneled more money into the process. Again the applications were rejected. Neto's mother finally gave up. She stopped pestering Neto and told her son that he should just send his aunt money to cover the cost of the surgery in San Salvador. But by then Neto had adopted hhis mother's worry that his tia's best chance at survival was in Los Angeles.

There was another option. Neto could hire a coyote to guide his aunt and Tomas across three treacherous borders and into the United States. Though it wasn't likely, Neto's anxiety convinced him that the payment would be traced back to him if they were caught entering illegally. For a week, Neto ran through the same pros-and-cons list, until the mangoes slipped into his mind, hovering above him like vultures do after a massacre. Without telling his mother, he paid the coyote. Neto wasn't very religious, but he lit a candle for his tia's safe crossing anyway.

As beautiful and expensive as the furniture in Steven and Neto's apartment was, it lacked practicality. The midcentury Danish teak chair only sat one, despite its flashy price tag. If Neto had been anyone else, Steven would have admitted what he felt inside: that it was silly to spend hundreds of dollars on a used chair that was uncomfortable to sit in. When guests came over, only a couple fit on their cramped love seat. The apartment was optimized for two, which was a problem. Tomas and his mother would be arriving in two weeks.

"They can't sleep on an air mattress in the office forever," Steven said.

"It'll only be for a couple of weeks. They'll adjust," Neto insisted.

"They deserve to feel comfortable."

"I'll go out and buy a futon, okay?" said Neto.

Where had Neto learned that money was a one-stop solution? Surely not from his parents, who were still paying off their mortgage and buying groceries in bulk. It could have been the university, with its private social clubs, fêtes, and an insistence that its alums could and should do whatever their hearts desired. The endless desire for more-more-more was celebrated, and Neto had gotten swept up in the rush.

Steven walked out of those halls with more skepticism than he'd entered with, though not out of naivete. He'd seen how life bent to those who swiped the right card, but also knew it was unpredictable and cruel.

His junior year, his godfather died suddenly. They'd been close growing up, spending every Saturday weed-whacking lawns for extra cash. When Steven went to college, his godfather sent him money every month, cash he didn't have to spare. "I can't be there to help you, so it's the least I can do," he'd said when Steven politely asked him to stop, knowing the toll extra shifts take on a body. After the funeral, Steven had nothing to show but an overdrawn checking account. Money couldn't replace the hours he'd given up by choosing Northeast prestige over a state school. When tragedy splintered a life, a credit card only went so far. Neto had to know that, somewhere deep inside.

Just in case he didn't, Steven prepared. On nights Neto worked overtime, Steven cleared out drawers for their guests' underwear and socks. From their linen closets, he dug out a couple of blankets he could part with. The wobbly towers of books came down, relocated to newly cleared bookshelves or donated to the local thrift store. The office began to resemble a guest bedroom. If Neto noticed the transformation, he didn't mention it.

"We should get to know each other," Steven insisted, even after Neto insisted that his aunt was open-minded, and understood how deeply they cared for each other. Tomas and Mami's faces appeared on the screen, grainy but unmistakably Neto's kin: eyes round as marbles, strong jaws, untamable black hair.

"Me llamo Steven," he said, drawing from the long-dry well of his high school Spanish. Tomas giggled, an airy and genuine sign of joy. Steven smiled, relieved to see excitement where he'd expected sadness.

"Los esperamos aqui," Steven continued. "En Los Angeles." Tomas gave him a thumbs-up, his finger skinny as a seedling. A child's hand. The connection was instant.

"This could work," Neto said when they'd said their goodbyes. Steven agreed. Eventually Neto bought the futon. With Steven's careful prodding, their apartment opened itself up slowly for the two exiles already on their way.

Tomas sat in the scratched-up plastic McDonald's booth somewhere in Arizona.

"Ah-ree-zoh-na," he'd been saying all day.

"Air-ih-zone-ah," Steven corrected him with a smile.

Neto looked around nervously, as if he expected to be confronted by a law enforcement agent in disguise. The coast was clear. They'd paid the coyote the second half of what they'd owed him—a whopping $8,000—before driving over to get Tomas a Happy Meal. He'd started begging for a drink as soon as they'd left the coyote's sight.

Ten minutes after finishing his hamburger, Tomas slid out of the booth and ran to the bathroom, ignoring Neto's concerned calls. He opened the closest stall, dropped to his knees in the same position he'd prayed in the desert, and began to throw up into the toilet. The hamburger was expelled by the third hurl, but Tomas kept dry-heaving as he knelt hunched over. He recognized his cousin's voice outside the stall, so he forced himself to stand up and walk to the sink to wash his hands. Neto placed a hand on Tomas's shoulder and led him to the car so they could head to Los Angeles.

Mami had passed away in Mexico. Neto said it must've been the illness, but Tomas knew that it wasn't. It'd been heartbreak, again. He wasn't sure how many times a heart could break, but he knew Mami's had reached its final rupture. Perhaps it was the fear that engulfed them as they walked through Mexican towns at night, hoping they wouldn't be robbed of everything they carried. It wasn't much: a few twenty-dollar bills and a dozen mangoes, the last batch for Neto until Mami recovered. But the fear was the same. Maybe one of her premonitions told her that she was going to die. The realization that her body would never be buried in Salvadoran soil, if buried at all, must've broken her heart for the last time.

Steven told Tomas they were passing the border into California with one of those shiny smiles that made his skin look even paler. The young boy tensed up, but as he looked out the window, he didn't see anything that screamed of danger, just gas stations and other cars on the highway beside them. Suddenly a ringing filled the car. Neto pushed a button in front of him and the ringing transformed into a woman's voice.

The woman was crying. Tomas knew it wasn't his mother's voice. He'd seen how Mami's eyes had rolled into the back of her head right before he'd closed them with shaking fingers. Yet the woman's voice had familiar inflections. She could be the ghost of Mami, Tomas thought.

Neto tried to soothe the ghost, telling her that it was all going to be okay. The ghost's sister hadn't been in contact for two weeks, and she couldn't get ahold of her nephew, which had to mean her sister had died. Neto soothed the voice on the speaker, saying he was so sorry for her loss. Once the tears had melted into soft sniffling, Neto hung up and told her that he'd see her soon.

Then the loud yelling in English began. Steven and Neto had both been speaking to Tomas in their oddly accented Spanish, Steven's more broken than his cousin's. But now Tomas felt himself disappear into the leather of the backseat.

Steven was yelling, quickly and angrily. Tomas's English was limited to what he learned in that one-room schoolhouse, on the rare days he went, and words lifted from the American action movies he loved so much. He caught tidbits of Steven's tirade. Liar. Selfish. Mother. Cousin. Mangoes. His cousin yelled back. Calm down. White lie. Dead. He heard his name come out of Steven's mouth.

"You're not going to tell your mom that you smuggled Tomas across the border and that he's living with you?"

After a few minutes, as if they'd tired themselves out, the two men fell into silence. Tomas extended a small hand to touch Steven's arm, and then Neto's. Neither of them could bear to turn and look at him. Out of a small plastic bag he'd miraculously held on to throughout his trip, he pulled out the only mango he'd saved. He'd refused to eat Neto's last mango, even as a crippling hunger had gnawed at his little belly.

At first it seemed like everything might work out. To help Tomas adjust, Neto took time off work. The trio played tourist in the city that was now the child's home, stuffing all the major landmarks into a day. After dinner, they swung by Whole Foods for that week's produce.

"Not as good as your mangoes," Neto said, a slice between his fingertips. Tomas nodded in agreement but continued chomping down on the soft flesh until only the fuzzy seed was left. He abandoned it on the white marble countertop, where it lay like a deep-sea creature washed ashore. Steven tossed it into the trash can before Neto had a chance to complain.

"Come on, Tomas." Steven ushered him into the living room to watch a movie. Neto sat in the uncomfortable Danish armchair and sent emails. Even when his manager acknowledged he was offline, he was online. Worried, Steven asked his boss if he could work from home until Tomas was in school. Once classes started, he made sure his schedule was free every afternoon, just in case Neto was pulled into a last-minute meeting. Yes, Steven wasn't related to the boy, but he was the one with the flexible work schedule. Plus, he'd really come to like the kid: his politeness, his excitement as he dropped him off at the school gate, his ability to laugh and play despite the unimaginable circumstances of his life. If he could make the transition a little easier, he would. It didn't matter that he wasn't blood.

The next time Steven left town, his phone buzzed in his pocket, catching him by surprise. It was the middle of the workday. Neto avoided personal calls while on the clock. Steven pulled the rented hatchback over, its wheels crunching against the ice blanketing the road shoulder. Frosty Michigan maples peered down as he picked up the phone, praying for good news.

"Hello? Tomas? Is everything okay?" Steven asked.

"Yes," Tomas said. "I just got home from school."

"Oh," Steven said, urging himself to keep his voice level. Relief would betray his hidden belief that their arrangement could go sour at any minute. "Is Neto around?"

"Yes," Tomas said. "But he's in the office. I got bored. So I called you."

"Have you seen your tio and tia yet?"

"No," Tomas said. Neto had said it was finally time to let his parents know the truth, and that he'd lay the groundwork while Steven was out of town.

"I'd like to speak to him, please."

"Is the Mitten as beautiful as your parents promised?" Neto asked.

"Even more," Steven said. "What are you up to?"

"Emails," Neto said. "Except answering emails at night isn't sustainable. I'm going to have to go into the office soon."

"We can't leave Tomas alone," Steven said.

Neto went quiet on the other end of the line, hurt at the assumption. He'd never be so careless, especially not with someone so young.

"We could find him a babysitter," Steven continued.

"I'd like to avoid anyone asking questions for now," Neto said.

"I'm sure your parents would be happy to watch him."

"I can't tell them everything. Not yet."

"They deserved to know weeks ago."

"I'm not having this conversation again. I'll figure something out," Neto promised.

"Can you give the phone back to Tomas?" Steven asked. Neto did.

"I miss you," Tomas said. If it was a difficult feeling to admit, his voice didn't show it. The words left his mouth as easily as a hymn or his ABCs.

"I miss you too," Steven admitted, as easily as Tomas had. "Be good."

Steven said goodbye and quickly hung up. If the call had gone a second longer, he would have made a confession he wasn't ready to: He loved Tomas. He felt protective of the child and didn't want anything to happen to him. This wasn't like the stretching, thinning love he felt for Neto, which he'd chosen to nurture despite its flaws. This felt more intense. Circumstance had pushed him closer to Tomas. Too close. The depth of his love scared him.

Steven shifted into drive, stomped on the gas pedal, and sped down the solitary road. He parked outside his godfather's house. The lawn was overgrown, but the leafless oak tree still stood strong. He imagined, for only a minute, that his godfather was inside, waiting for him to knock on the door. No one gets to choose their family, Steven thought. Loved ones will disappoint you, and leave you, and there's no opting out of the pain that comes when they do. Perhaps that was his lifeline. If he pulled away from Tomas now, he might free himself from the vines of a family tree cinching tight against his chest.

Before the new owner could step outside and shatter his fantasy, Steven rushed back home. Desperately, he needed to get back to the quiet street he'd grown up on, with its red mailboxes and crumbing sidewalks. There, in the warmth of their cramped living room, his parents waited patiently for him to return. The oak is still alive, he'd tell them, and they'd know he wasn't talking about a tree at all.

Tomas missed Steven, but he didn't mention it because he knew Neto would get upset. The one time he'd asked his primo why Steven wasn't living in the apartment with them anymore, Neto told him that Steven had moved out. Neto struggled to find the right word in Spanish for breakup, trying quebramos and rompimos and terminamos until Tomas eventually understood.

The evening Steven flew back, Neto made every excuse to cancel dinner with his parents. "Aren't you tired from your flight?" "We'll be driving back so late at night." When a babysitter showed up at the front door, Steven understood why. Dinner dragged on, and when the night ended without a mention of Tomas, the relationship was over. Steven packed his bags and moved back to Michigan two weeks later.

The distance hadn't stopped Tomas from video-chatting Steven. He'd sneak into the bathroom, usually when Neto was still at work, and call Steven. The conversations flowed calmly, like the river in Guazapa before a major storm, as Steven pulled his Spanish out of his mouth slowly and deliberately.

Their ritual always came first. Hola, they'd tell each other. Have you seen your tia yet? Steven would ask. No, Tomas would always reply. Steven would shake his head, or roll his eyes, or let out a hushed curse. Then he'd ask about school, and the conversation would go on from there until Tomas heard Neto coming.

One afternoon, about six months after he'd moved in, Tomas heard the front of the apartment open. He quickly hung up on Steven and stuffed his phone under his pillow. Neto hadn't explicitly forbidden the calls, but it was his house, so Tomas wanted to keep him happy. Neto knocked on the door twice before walking into the bedroom.

"I have a surprise for you in the kitchen," he said. Barefoot, Tomas quietly followed his cousin.

There wasn't a knife, bowl, or cutting board in sight. On the shiny, sanitized, spotless white marble countertop, Neto had left a neat row of items: gardening gloves, a spade, a bag of fertilizer, and a watering can. The child was confused, until Neto handed him the sapling he was hiding behind his back and told him to plant it later that afternoon.

The label read MANGO. Tomas cried for the first time in this new country, an intense fear spreading from his throat all the way down to his green thumb.

**TRY
AGAIN**

A S I READ DAD'S EULOGY, MY mind was on the FedEx delivery that'd bring him back to me.

"My father was a thoughtful man," I said. "In his poems and in his life, he sought to understand people's complexity. He didn't believe that people were good or bad. He was most interested in gray areas. With generosity, he saw the world's ugliness and tried shining a kind gloss on it wherever he could."

"That was a really beautiful speech," Rafael said. We weren't together at that point, but he'd driven down from Davis for the funeral, even though I hadn't asked him to.

"Thank you," I said. I didn't mean it. We both knew the eulogy was too kind, too convenient. More fluff than anything.

At the reception, everyone wanted to share happy memories about Dad, but I kept replaying what'd happened the night before. A SyncALife employee visited the morgue and drilled a small hole into Dad's head. They took a chunk of gray matter back to their facilities, reanimated a few of the dead cells, and implanted them in a robot. It all had to be done before Dad was lowered into the ground at Forest Lawn. No one knew I was waiting for my purchase. I couldn't admit I'd already spent my ten-thousand-dollar inheritance.

Dad wasn't a famous poet, but he was respected by those who knew his work. My whole life I'd heard how vulnerable he was on the page, though I'd spent years searching for that frankness. Guests kept coming up to me to say how much he had adored me.

"He did love me," I finally admitted. It was all I could muster as I ushered people out of the two-bedroom Highland Park home I grew up in.

"Call if you need anything," Rafael ventured. He wanted to say more, but I told him it wasn't the right time.

Before I'd made it back inside, I caught the bright glare of headlights in my periphery and heard the soft crackle of loose asphalt under tires. A deliveryman, his paunch heavy and pushing against his shirt like Dad's had, made me sign for the package before grabbing it from the back of the truck.

I tore through the tape and Styrofoam peanuts, cradling the robot in my arms. It was as small as the nutcracker Dad put on the mantel in late November. Faint paint strokes, handcrafted onto the tinny metal, conjured my father's lumberjack beard and widow's peak, his color-blocked polos and khaki slacks. The robot had his face. Its limbs were limp and turned into its body, as if curled in pain. The instruction manual said that once it was powered up, it'd be able to carry ten times its weight, like an ant. I gently stretched its limbs until finally it stood on its own.

"Hello," I said, as instructed.

The robot didn't respond. A glowing blue line ran across a tiny screen on its chest. It reminded me of the vital monitors in the hospital, sans the beeping. I reread the instruction manual, to see if I'd done something wrong. All SyncALife robots required a few weeks for the artificial intelligence software to fully develop, so their linguistic capacity was limited at first, but they were supposed to respond from the moment they first booted up.

"Dad, can you hear me?" I said. The robot stirred. The sounds didn't coalesce into words, but the babble and gurgling were unmistakable. It was Dad's voice.

Though he wasn't famous, Dad ended up on several syllabi, including one for a required Chicano Literature course I'd taken as a college freshman. The professor was a fan, and he assigned a poem from Dad's first collection, *Sins of War and Man:*

nightmare
> *blood bursts from my chest*
> *muddies dirt I slept on*
> *soaks comrades sleeping still as restless night*

> *blood bursts from my chest*
> *springs like holy fountain*
> *into mouth of the Lempa River*

> *blood floods the bank*
> *bodies of dead indios, guerrilleros, children,*
> *float in endless red River Styx*

> *covered in blood from my sinner's chest*

The class was strange and awkward, not least because I was encountering a man I didn't recognize, one who was open and honest about who he'd been before he became my father. A quieter, calmer man. The night he died, in a fugue of disbelief I reread the poem, re-creating the uncanny encounter. It was like meeting a younger, more naïve man. One who could face what he'd experienced, so long as his son wasn't in the room.

The cruel thing about grief is that it doesn't care where you are or how you're feeling. Out of nowhere, a random memory descends, even if your mind has been running a hundred miles an hour over the hundred things on your to-do list. The memory could be of the most mundane, ordinary day, and still, it'll send an ancient sadness through you. The sort of sadness you imagine humans have felt since creation, but that you never imagined you could experience so deep inside.

That's how it was with Dad in the days after I buried him. There I was, listening to my manager explain that he'd love to give me a raise, especially after my loss, but that the call center simply didn't have the budget. I was about to say I really needed the money, and that I didn't know how I'd pay the bills on my own, when, boom: A memory. Out of nowhere. Shell-shocked me. My manager stared me down when I went silent for too long, lost in thought.

"Okay. Thank you," I said, my financial situation unresolved.

The memory was from when I was nine. Dad and I went back to his hometown of Santa Tecla to launch the Spanish translation of *Sins of War and Man.* It was the first time he and I had been to El Salvador together, the first trip after Mom left, taking the buffer between us with her.

All summer I'd begged him for the Nintendo 64. There was nothing I loved more than playing *Pokémon Stadium* at a friend's house, and all I wanted was to be able to do that every day, but Dad refused to buy me one. When we got to Santa Tecla and pulled into the parking lot of the gated colonia where Dad had grown up, he opened up his suitcase and pulled out a brand-new console, still in the box.

I thought he was surprising me, but it turned out the N64 was for a comrade's kid. Dad said he'd appreciate it more than me. I went on to spend the whole summer with that boy, playing *Pokémon Stadium* and *Star Fox 64,* and we eventually kissed, which led to all the yelling, but that wasn't the point. Dad was dead and he'd gifted a Nintendo 64 to a kid who otherwise couldn't have afforded it. Grief made it a tender memory.

The SyncALife robot was waiting for me where I'd left it. I

figured I'd try communicating with it again, since the purchase was supposed to stave off the loneliness and grief that'd seeped in anyway. I missed Dad.

"How are you feeling, Dad?" I asked. It was one of the phrases suggested in the instructional manual as a way of speeding up linguistic development.

"Meh cien toe leek um days per tan dough fromage dream," it muttered. "Eye om nut sheer key in Aries too."

"I don't understand you, Dad," I said. It'd been speaking like this for days, in a jumbled-up soup of sounds that almost sounded like words but didn't coalesce into anything I could decipher.

"Meh cien toe leek um days per tan dough fromage dream," it repeated.

"Okay, Dad," I said. "We'll talk later."

SyncALife had a refund policy on the off chance the robot never acquired language. All I had to do was flip the switch on its foot, verbally confirm that I wanted to terminate the service, and hit the switch again. A part of me wanted to do it then. It had Dad's face, but not much else. Dad was still dead, I still missed him, and even though the robot mumbled in a register that was unmistakably Dad's, I couldn't talk to him like I wanted to. Plus, I needed the money.

Hope is dangerous, but priceless when it pays off, so I didn't send the robot back.

When the paramedics called to say that Dad had a fainting episode he was lucky to have woken up from, I stuffed all my clothes into the trunk of my Prius and drove down from Davis for good.

Rafael asked why I'd willingly put myself back in a bad situation. Dad wasn't happy that I'd moved in with Rafael. He stopped helping me with tuition and rent, in retribution for "abandoning" him, and though it was a fair price to pay to be away from everything I'd endured under his care, it still stung.

Rafael had a point, but I told him I had no choice. Even then I had the sense that my decision might lead to a breakup, which was especially ironic since I'd come out to Dad to prove that I was serious about our relationship. Rafael had never questioned who he was or who he loved. He wanted to be with me, so I pretended my soul was a ribbon like his, instead of an ugly knot.

If I could be around to help Dad if he passed out again— well, of course I would. I've never been a bad son. In my own estimations, at least.

Dad was a subdued version of his old self then, which meant that he still got angry with me but in a passive-aggressive way, complaining about my reckless left turns or the music I played during our drives to the doctor. He didn't shout or throw things, but I still felt his frustration.

To avoid him, I shut the door to my room and watched amateur interior designers give house tours online. Their living rooms didn't seem lived-in, and they all stole ideas from the same sources: *Kinfolk*, IKEA catalogs, overused Pinterest boards. But there was something pristine and aspirational about their homes. They were quiet, minimalist spaces. So different than the home I'd grown up in.

During one of these videos, I got an ad. *SyncALife is a state-of-the-art technology that preserves the memories of your loved ones after they've transitioned out of this life and into the next. Compact and easy to set up, you'll be able to bring your loved ones on all of life's big adventures.* A pair of Stanford grads conceptualized of SyncALife as a malleable, personally adjustable robot that'd mimic the behaviors of the deceased. Initially the company developed it for children's pets. Dogs, cats, and hamsters were easier to "bring back to life," since their personalities were less complex than a human's. But soon it was clear that the real moneymaker would be technology capable of imitating a dead parent or grandparent. They figured out how to reanimate brain cells and coupled them with AI software. Customers' orders were based on their loved ones, but the company couldn't guarantee they'd be identical to the deceased, a disclaimer buried in fine print.

I found the hidden caveat when I was placing my order, but it didn't seem so bad. There'd been so many versions of Dad: poet, coach, caretaker, hothead, protector. They say the house always wins, but grief respects logic as much as a gambler does. I was willing to take my chances.

Even though the robot still wasn't talking, I liked having it around. Its babbling filled the room, giving me white noise to stew in, the only distraction from my thoughts. Still, I was desperate to hear Dad, to talk to him. He hadn't been a very good texter, and he never sent voice notes, so I returned to the only place that contained his voice. His books.

From *Sins of War and Man*:

cruel reminder
>   *more than the break of dawn*
>   *or vinyl singing in an empty room*
>   *or phantom carcass in bedsheets' folds*

>   *our son reminds me of you*
>   *of the cruelties that left*
>   *the room empty*
>   *the sheets phantoms*
>   *dawn broken like me*

Dad always said that the poet is separate from the speaker of his poems, but he was only half-right. The resentment in that poem, presumably written at some point after my mother had had enough, was real. He tried to overcome it. He really did. He stepped in and did what he needed to. He got a tenure-track job, kept me fed, never missed a soccer game or choir recital. But I'd never heard the voice on the page. So meek, so reflective. Maybe that was how he wanted to live, somewhere between a silence and a shout. Our desire to be good must count for something, even when we misstep. Even when we fail.

After a few days of gurgled sounds, Dad put words together. Baby talk pulled from the two languages he'd wrapped his tongue around in his lifetime.

"No say woo eye em," he said, this time as I was clearing out his room. This version of Dad didn't need cologne or polo shirts. "There ease so men y bags in hair. Decking son?"

"There's a lot of stuff to get rid of, Dad," I said, assuming he understood me. The instruction manual said to speak to the robot as I would anyone else.

I tied a white trash bag to the bed frame and began to throw things away. Dad watched from the doorway until I walked over, crouched down, and took his aluminum hand in mine. Still hunched over, I pulled him into the room. He toddled at my side and let me guide him.

"Can you help me out?" I asked. It didn't seem like he recognized the piles of objects in the room as his own, but if they really had put Dad's brain matter into this robot, there had to be a way of drawing out recognition. I handed Dad a bottle of Nautica cologne, which he almost dropped. It was a third of his size, a cheap fragrance he'd bought at Ross and used often. The phantom scent of perfume and sweat assailed me.

"Wise diss?" he asked. SyncALife Dad held the bottle out in front of him as if it were a piece of space junk. Fascinating, but foreign. He held on to it for a while, which had to mean something.

"How about these shirts, Dad?"

I handed him a small stack of polos that used to press against his stomach. He tossed them aside.

"Dent want dos."

We went like this for the rest afternoon: me handing my dead father's stuff to his reincarnated robot and taking his reaction as guidance. I was guessing—it wasn't always clear whether or not Dad liked whatever he was holding—but it felt like he was choosing what to throw away and what to keep, taking the burden off me. In the back of my head, I knew it didn't matter. Dad didn't need anything. He was dead. I should have thrown it all away.

That night, I went to the grocery store to get some vegetables. I couldn't remember the last time I'd put something green in my stomach. Probably at the post-burial reception. When I put my debit card into the machine, the cashier looked at me apologetically.

"It says it's been declined. You can try again."

I shook my head, pulled out my credit card, and swiped it, before rushing to the car in embarrassment. The receipt was less than thirty dollars, but I'd taken over my father's mortgage. Paying it that month had wiped out my checking account.

At home, watching spinach sizzle and shrink in the saucepan, I realized I couldn't drag my feet any longer. My father spent the better part of his adult life paying off the property, and he'd been so proud to call himself a homeowner. Selling it was off the table. I'd have to supplement my income somehow. The call center wouldn't cut it.

"What am I gonna do, Dad?" I asked him, though I had an

obvious solution in mind. One he would have hated.

"Meh cientoe leek um days per tan dough fromage dream," he muttered. "Eye om nut sheer key in Aries too."

"I don't know what you're saying, Dad. Can you try again? Please, Dad. Porfa."

"Meh siento like I'm desper tanto from a dream. Eye um not sheer quien Aires tu."

"You feel, what? A dream?" Dad was getting closer and closer to words I understood.

"Me siento like I'm despertando from a dream. I am not sure quien eres tu,"

"I'm your son," I cried. "Soy tu hijo, Dad."

"May soon. Mai sun. My son?" he asked. "My son."

Dad sat there watching as I ate forkfuls of spinach. It was impossible to tell whether he understood what having a son entailed, but my gut told me he did. SyncALife warned that they had no way of knowing what details from life their AI would cling to, but I hoped he'd at least remember what it meant to be my father. The good parts, the happy moments, at least.

Before Dad knew I was attracted to men, our relationship was normal. Or, more accurately, as normal a relationship possible between an emotionally repressed former guerrillero and his son.

He was an unexceptional sort of man in that he loved me but couldn't say it plainly. Instead, he did the sorts of things too many men get away without doing: supporting me financially, coaching my recreational soccer team for a couple years, talking to me about condoms and sex and the way a child can derail your life if you're not ready for it. It was a kind of love, but not the kind I wanted.

What I wanted was the unconditional, explicitly stated, I'll-die-for-you sort of love Dad had shown the men he spent his twenties with.

The guerrilleros were working to establish a freer El Salvador with more political space for debate and fewer kidnappings and killings. But to stage such a war meant taking to the overgrown hillsides of the rainforest, where they spent days evading government soldiers and planning counterattacks. As the vines nipped at their ankles, Dad and the other men slept in hammocks next to each other. To pass the time, they read verses of poetry out loud. They embraced, cooked together, and found solace not simply in their cause, but also in each other.

That was love between men. Dad was capable of it, but never showed it to me. As a boy, I figured it'd come one day—when I was old enough and man enough to understand the world as he did. When I learned that most of Dad's comrades had been murdered in the war, I understood him better. If every "I love you" conjured memories of those I'd lost, I'd struggle to say it too.

That didn't make his hesitation hurt less, and it definitely didn't prepare me for his reaction when I revealed my relationship with Rafael. Despite all he'd been through, I never imagined he'd choose violence and call it love.

The week Dad began speaking in full sentences, Rafael sent a message saying he was moving down to Los Angeles to start a new job. He chose email, I guessed, because it'd be easier for me to ignore than calls or texts. Rafael respected boundaries, and though I did miss him, I didn't respond immediately, telling myself I was busy teaching Dad about the world.

SyncALife claimed its robots were shaped by fixed processes— algorithms and biology—but they also didn't dissuade customers who were convinced they were purchasing better versions of the people they'd known. Online, users hocked tips and tricks for raising loved ones that would be slightly more reliable, a bit less impulsive. And though I was skeptical, the possibilities made me dizzy. Why lie? I'd do anything for a dad that was kinder than the dead one had been.

Dad and I spent evenings revisiting activities we hadn't done together since before Mom left. On the shaggy white rug, we tossed down Uno cards, laughing when we'd curse the other with a skip or wild card. We went for walks around the neighborhood, and Dad would stop to pet a dog if we encountered one. We tried new activities too. We watched *27 Dresses*, *13 Going on 30*, and old reruns of *Fear Factor*. I put on *Brokeback Mountain* one night but felt immediately overwhelmed by the task of explaining the film. I shut it off before Heath Ledger stepped into the tent.

Mostly I answered his questions: who I was, how to turn on the television, how rain happened. He never asked anything too serious, but with every question, he got closer to asking questions I wouldn't know how to answer: what he was like when he was alive, how our relationship had been.

Before I knew it, another month's bills were due. To distract him for the evening, I sat Dad on the couch to watch *Saturday Night Live*. It was a show he'd liked in life, and as the cold open began, I could tell he was enjoying it. Proof that he's himself again, I told myself.

I went into my room and got onto all fours, sticking a hand deep underneath my bed frame until my fingers touched the slim edges of a box. Dust covered the top, and I ran a finger through it, leaving a greasy line. I opened it and carefully laid the black wig on my mattress. Next to it, I unfolded the sequined purple body suit.

A familiar routine followed, but it'd been months since I'd done it—ever since I moved back in with Dad—so it felt exciting in a way it hadn't since the very beginning. I combed the wig, getting every strand in place. Though I left my boxers on, I pulled on my dick and tucked it in between my thighs before slipping into the one-piece, one leg at a time. The glittering fabric was tight on my hips and chest, and I turned in a circle, feeling the bell-bottoms sway at my ankles. Once the hairnet was tight against my skull, I put the wig on and there I was: Selena under the lights of the Houston Astrodome in '95. Smiling, shining, precious as a gem.

The camboy website had saved my password, so logging in was easy. I made sure my bedroom door was locked, then I hit the "Broadcast Now" button. The chat room filled up quickly. There were ten, then fifteen, then thirty people watching. I began to strip off my clothes, slowly, and as more of my skin showed, more usernames popped up in the chat. *Take it off sexy*, one user typed, after donating a hundred tokens. I listened and pulled the jumpsuit down to my knees. I was hard.

My boxer briefs were tight and black, and the wig swung against the waistband. I ran my fingers through the strands, over my nipples, down my body, and continued taking men's requests. The tips were flowing, and the idea of all these anonymous men with their eyes on me turned me on. *Would love to worship that cock*, a user wrote once my underwear was around my ankles.

When I turned the camera off, the jumpsuit splattered with my cum, I didn't feel disgusted at myself. I'd made the money I needed for the bills, and I felt beautiful.

From Dad's second book, *Genesis*:

1 Corinthians 6:19–20
for Flaco
   The body is not a temple

But a cage: skeleton dome
Tender muscle base, fluttering heart

When the bomb bursts
Flaco's cage shatters
Shards of marrow in
Bloody pools of flesh

His fluttering heart loose,
Ground-bound canary,
In civil war mines

In a jewelry box under Dad's bed, I discovered a photograph of him and Flaco in their school uniforms, his arm draped across his classmate's skinny shoulder. They're both smiling, without an inch of distance between them. He looks happy, happier than I can remember. I did what I wish Dad had done when he was alive. I framed the picture and put it in our living room, out in the open for all to see.

Camming brought in enough money to pay the bills as long as I put shows on regularly, so I quit my job. Guilt seeped in briefly, but not because I'd turned to sex work. I'd sustained myself by camming in the months I was financially cut off, but doing it inside my childhood home with Dad in the house—even this growing, learning version of him—felt dirty.

I did it anyway and invested in new wigs and outfits to replace the ones I'd gotten rid of when I moved back home. In a short bob and silk slip dress, I was Hollywood glamour. A pink wig, corset, and plaid miniskirt made me a pop-star daydream. For the camera, I became half a dozen different women. Sometimes I didn't wear a costume. Logging on in nothing but my boxer briefs was also liberating.

Online, I could be whoever I wanted to be and there'd always be admirers. By being everyone, I was no one, and the anonymity in that lack of identity was freeing.

I was in the middle of a show when Rafael's contact photo popped up—a shot I'd taken of him sitting in a sea of poppies—so I let the phone buzz. When I'd finished wiping cum off my fingers with a tissue, I called him back. He was glad that I'd finally responded to his email.

"Would you want to grab lunch?" he asked. I told him I'd think about it.

The sound of audience laughter came from the living room, so I changed into a new pair of underwear and joined Dad on the couch. He sat silently, occasionally turning from the sketches. Whenever Dad spoke, the blue line on his screen spiked, but as we watched, it flatlined. It was strange, because when we'd watched *SNL* together before he died, he always had commentary.

"You should watch the old stuff," Dad had said once. He was glaring at Lady Gaga's backup dancers, in their skirts and gold corsets. "I used to watch it when I lived in Miami. So much better than this shit. Hans and Franz—we want to pump you up!—in those accents. Even that guy who dressed as a woman. Church Lady. Even that was funny. This stuff . . ." He'd trailed off.

That evening, though, he laughed occasionally, a deep and hearty joy that sent a small quiver through his aluminum limbs. The laugh was the same one he'd always had, but one I had heard rarely. Dad seemed remade. The sensitivity and curiosity readers had found in his poetry—I saw it in this version of him. I could come out again.

"I'm bisexual," I said. I figured it'd be best to say it as simply as possible.

"No entiendo."

"Romantically, I like men and women."

"You would marry either, hombre o mujer?"

"Yes."

"Okay."

Dad turned back to the television. The show had ended, and the host was saying the final goodbye with the cast behind him. As the credits rolled, the cast members embraced each other, some dancing to the audience's applause. I had an urge to hug Dad, but it was a stupid thought. He was a robot. He'd be cold against my skin.

I came out to Dad, the first time, because I was in love. A giddy, can't-get-my-mind-off-you kind of love. The sort of love I'd only ever felt for women before, and that I assumed I'd never feel for a man.

The boys before Rafael had come and gone in a flurry of headless torso pictures and three A.M. "u up?" texts. We met in the dark, in the backseat of their cars or the cramped space of their dorm rooms, but it never amounted to much. I convinced myself that I didn't actually love men. I just loved the feeling of their bodies on mine, or inside me, or slick on my skin.

But Rafael was different. We met the same way—online, under the pretense of sex. Soon, though, he was coming around often. He'd text me to ask where I was studying, and then would join with an iced coffee I hadn't asked for but gratefully accepted. His love was unflinching, unashamed.

I wanted more with Rafael, a real relationship and maybe a future, so I cliff-dived into the conversation I'd been fearing.

Here's what I remember: I said what I had to. My hands were trembling, so I gripped my knees. Dad said nothing, until he said no. No, he said. I don't believe it. I didn't raise a maricón.

I reassured him it had nothing to do with him, that I couldn't help what I felt. I was about to tell him about Rafael when suddenly he left. Slammed the door behind him and left for a walk. I thought he'd left to clear his mind, and that when he returned, we'd ignore what I'd said. I was okay with the idea that Dad would ignore who I really was as a way of coping. As long as he knew, that'd be fine.

But when he came back, he was still fuming. He came up to where I was sitting on the couch, loomed over me, and stood over me with fists clenched. It was so unexpected, and I could have probably struck first, but I didn't. I covered my head with my hands and took the blow. I was crying by then. He only hit me once, before shutting himself in his bedroom. I could smell his cologne, even after he'd left the living room.

"I remember the house," Dad said to me one day, about three months after he'd been delivered.

"Really?" I asked. He'd had moments like these, where his past came back to him in snippets. The man I buried was remerging, which brought flares of the joy I'd been seeking.

"What do you remember about this house?"

"There was a hole once in the drywall. I fixed it myself because I didn't want to pay a contractor."

It was a random memory, but it was true. He'd made the hole himself, when I was living in Davis, though I imagined his fist against the drywall for months after he told me about it. When I moved back, I worried that he'd be violent again, but he never was. Maybe he regretted his actions. Either that or the illness had made him too weak. Maybe I'd ask, someday.

"What do you miss most about El Salvador?" I asked instead. It was a question I'd always wanted to ask, but that had felt too loaded. Now, with this second chance, it slipped out easily.

"My family," he said. "The farm my mother grew up on."

"She moved to Santa Tecla during the war, didn't she?"

"The war?" he asked.

The past was suddenly a hot iron in my throat. The most unfathomable cruelty of war is that the winners—those who survive—are forced to keep living. I changed the subject.

"Do you remember living alone, here in California?" I asked.

"Did I live alone?" Dad said.

"No," I lied. "I've always been here with you."

Rafael and I met at Guisados on Cesar Chavez. The conversation was easy, both of us reaching for the relationship we'd had before the breakup. I apologized for the ways I'd sunk the relationship: saying long-distance would never work, failing to admit that I hadn't outgrown the shame my father instilled in me, quitting because things got hard. By the end of lunch, I knew we were getting back together. The love that had been there—dormant, untouched—blazed.

We stumbled through my front door, our hands interlocked, and in our hurry to get into my bedroom, Rafael knocked Dad over.

"Shit," he said. "I'm sorry."

"It's okay," Dad said. He lifted himself off the floor, his joints whirring quietly. He stood just below Rafael's knees. Awkwardly, I introduced them, though my tongue felt heavy. I hadn't told Dad that Rafael and I were seeing each other again.

"Nice to meet you," Rafael said.

"Likewise," Dad said. "I'll get out of your way." There it was again: the newfound kindness I'd secretly hoped for. It felt good, but unnerving, like reading one of his poems for the first time.

In my room, with his torso pressed against me, all I could focus on was Rafael's body. His cock inside me, the way his hips knocked against my ass. Sweat dripped down from his temple, and as he leaned over me, pressing his cheek against mine, the slickness made its way onto my skin. When we were done, we lay in bed together, silent, but smiling into each other's bodies.

"You must have spent a small fortune on him," Rafael said.

"Ten grand," I admitted, only because I knew he wouldn't judge me, even if he disagreed with my choice. Meeting Dad must've conjured the horror stories I'd told about him, the same way Dad's voice triggered those memories for me sometimes.

"He's sweet," Rafael said.

"He doesn't care who I date anymore. He's changed in that way."

Dad liked what I liked, and passively followed my lead. For the first time ever, I was the man of the house, a responsibility I'd never asked for. We were getting along, but despite what I told Rafael, I couldn't enjoy the new dynamic. It felt like Dad hadn't ever really returned.

"Sorry I didn't tell you Rafael was coming over," I told Dad after Rafael left.

"You're an adult. Sos adulto," he said, which was true. The anger, yelling, reprimands, ugly stares—none of it came. "Just be safe."

I had always wanted Dad to be this way, measured and slow to anger, but now that he was, it made me feel as if the person I spoke to daily wasn't Dad at all. Without the short fuse, and the desire for control, how could I pretend that this was my father?

According to the online forums, SyncALife users who felt that their loved ones were missing essential pieces of their personality could use mementos to teach their robots about who they used to be. I knew what I had to do.

Every night, Dad and I read a couple of pages from his collections. I showed him the photograph of Flaco and one of my mother.

"Do you remember writing that?" I asked Dad after we were done reading for the evening.

"Sí. Yes," he said. "Santa Tecla, 1989." Or, "Miami, 1994." Or, "Los Angeles, 2006."

He never said more than that—the place and year where he'd written the lines I read out loud—but it was reassuring to know he remembered.

The online forums were right: His personality was coming back. He scolded me for buying fast food so often, saying the grease was showing in my cheeks. I ignored him, as I had learned to do as a teenager, but began throwing the bags in the trash bins outside so he wouldn't see them. We still watched *Saturday Night Live* every weekend, but he became pickier with other shows. Rom-coms and reality television no longer interested him. Part of me thought he'd insult me to my face, saying that what I watched was inane, childish, girly. Instead, he silently got off the couch to wander the house. Our conversations became slimmer, more timid.

Still, I liked reading to him. Even when it was clear that Dad could read for himself, I insisted we flip through his books together. We went chronologically, and as we reached the end of his last collection—published a year before his death—I found myself rationing the poems. Instead of two or three a night, I only read one, and despite the slowed-down pace, we got to the end of the book. The poem that closed it out was about me.

The room was still. The refrigerator's muted buzz came from the kitchen, louder than the shallow pulsing of my own chest.

"Qué bello, mijo." Dad struggled to get the sentence out.

"Your words," was all I could muster.

"Te quiero," Dad said. I stayed quiet, so he tried again. "I love you."

Dad had loved me when he was alive, even when he had hated parts of me, but he almost never put his feelings into words, despite being a writer. Hearing them now, the syllables sweet and silky, sent a pang through me.

Again, I resisted the urge to hug him. It'd ruin the illusion. Not the illusion of love, because the love was true, but the illusion that Dad was the same Dad I'd grown up with. He wasn't, neither in body nor in spirit. Not fully, at least. It didn't matter then. Sinking into my delusion, I smiled at him.

"I love you, Dad."

With Rafael back in my life, there was finally another person to invest energy into. He and Dad got along fine, and though Dad didn't have much to say to him, he didn't flinch when he came over. I took it as another sign that Dad wasn't as cruel as he'd been in life.

Loving Dad had always been hard, and loving Rafael was easy. Maybe that's why I ended up camming more than I needed to. If nothing else, I could show this new version of Dad love by providing for him: a roof to sleep under, a cable subscription to quell his boredom. He required less of my time, and though Rafael kept me busy, I had the urge to give, so I spent hour after hour dressing up and getting naked; touching myself and climaxing to the chimes of tips being sent my way.

Then it happened.

A black bob grazed my shoulders. Sequins fell down to my knees, and small circles of makeup gave my cheeks a perpetual blush. Giving 1920s-flapper-girl glamour was intoxicating as always. Rafael was on my bed, out of frame, watching me perform.

Hiking the hem up to my hips, I pulled down my underwear but kept the dress on. My eyes were closed, and I had my hand wrapped around my cock, stroking it slowly but deliberately, ensuring that viewers could see my palm slide down my shaft.

The door must have creaked, but, because I was engrossed in the moment, only the sounds of the chat rang in my ears. When I heard Dad, it was too late to cover up or feign an excuse.

"What the fuck are you doing?" Dad spit out.

What could I say? Even if I'd managed to formulate my panic, embarrassment, and shame into words, it wouldn't have been louder than Dad's shouts.

"In my house? What is this bullshit? You're dressed up as a girl. The boyfriend, whatever. Sure. But this? This? I didn't raise you to be such a sissy, hijueputa."

It was the first time Dad had yelled, but it was unmistakable. His voice boomed, and though he stood only slightly larger than a doll or action figure, I felt tiny.

"Mare in con," he said, stumbling on the word, trying to find language for whatever he felt at the sight of me, exposed and dressed like a woman. Immediately I knew what he was trying to say.

"Mar y cone.

"Mary con.

"Maricón."

He kept repeating the slur, louder and louder. The word became unbearable. The door was still open, so I took him by the head and tossed him outside into the hallway before slamming the door. Unphased, he kept yelling, the words barely muffled.

I slipped out of my dress, tossed my wig onto my bed, and swung the door open. Wearing nothing but my underwear, I stepped toward him. Rafael watched over my shoulder.

Dad paused, taking in the sight of me chulón, my skin exposed in a way he hadn't seen since I was a toddler. Quickly, without hesitation or appeals to his logic, I wrapped my hand around his leg and turned him upside down. I flipped the switch on the bottom of his foot.

A distorted version of Dad's voice came from the robot, like he was speaking to me from the other end of a long tunnel.

"Are you sure you want to terminate your SyncALife?"

I dropped him.

Grief had made me bring Dad back, and though I'd tried my best to meld him into the father I'd always wanted, he'd found a way to hate me anyway. It was my own doing, but I was still angry at him for all the ugly words, all the ugly actions. I looked to Rafael for guidance, but his face reflected what I knew: the choice was mine, and mine alone.

"I'm sure," I said, grabbing Dad.

I pressed my thumb to the switch. The LED lights in his eyes went out. The house went quiet. Rafael approached me from behind, wrapping his arms around my waist. His chest was fleshy and warm against me. I lowered myself to the floor, cradling the robot in my arms. Rafael's balmy breath tickled my ear as he whispered that he loved me, and that everything would be okay.

Even if I regretted our second try, it felt wrong to see Dad die once more. How cruel, that I still loved him, and that I'd miss him again.

AN
ALTERNATE
HISTORY OF
EL SALVADOR
OR PERHAPS
THE WORLD

THE BONES WERE FOUND BY ACCIDENT, but the Salvadoran government wasted no opportunity. The Minister of Culture sent a telegram to the national press, and though the journalist tasked with writing the article had more questions, the official refused to elaborate. Swallowing his questions like a spoonful of cough syrup, the journalist wrote the story he was instructed to.

The bones had been excavated as part of a broader attempt to preserve the country's cultural patrimony. The president had decreed the dig, and though no one had expected bones, that's what paleontologists discovered. In the land of volcanoes, they'd found a dinosaur. It was a feat of archaeology. Almost all the bones were intact and the museum in the capital would be able to display them all together, bringing the long-dead predator from the Cretaceous back to life. His teeth were rumored to be as large as a child's forearm. He must've towered above where the annona trees grazed the sky. El Salvador was a growing, peaceful, united nation. Patriotic citizens had uncovered evidence of an equally powerful and grandiose ancestor.

When the fossilized skeleton demanded a name, the choice was obvious. No name was more appropriate for such a majestic beast, one whose bones would be proof of the nation's importance. *Maximilianodon*. A mouthful, but appropriate. The etymology: teeth like the general, teeth like the president, teeth glorious teeth.

President Maximiliano Hernández Martínez reportedly loved the name and felt honored that a piece of national history would be his namesake. His teeth were not quite as large as the dinosaur's, he'd joked at a state dinner, but he wasn't afraid to bite if things got ugly. He was a military man, after all. Drawing a little bit of blood once in a while was part of the job.

Once the bones had been fully extracted and cleaned, they had to be transported to the capital. They were carefully loaded into trucks, secured with a combination of rope, bricks, and sandbags that would ensure the bones shifted as little as possible. The truck beds were covered with sturdy canvas tarps that made the fossils look like a badly wrapped gift. Large stretches of highway were worn-down and patchy, so the bones only moved a few dozen miles a day.

The morning before the drivers left, state-sponsored newspapers published the route. The headline read "Come See the Bones, While You Can!" And people did. They scurried from their adobe homes, nestled among trees and next to plots of land they farmed for larger, richer families, and found their way to the bit of road the trucks would glide past on. Everyone wanted a view of the monstrous dinosaur, especially since most couldn't afford a day off or a ride to the city. The procession was well attended, drawing crowds as large as those that gathered during Holy Week and the Christmas holidays. People stood by, whooping as the procession went by, even though the dusty tarp obscured their vision. Observers filled their heads with their own ideas of what the dinosaur looked like, their imagination revealing what remained hidden from them.

A group of pious farmers decided to follow the trucks, hoping they'd see the bones at some point. If they didn't start barefoot, their shoes soon fell apart. The bottoms of their feet split and hardened as they followed the procession, which continued to move glacially. By the time the bones arrived at the capital — where an expensive spectacle of a celebration was held — the caravan of followers had dissipated. None made it to the homecoming.

As exciting and well publicized as the bones were, there were people who knew the truth. Even those with the resources to reach a broad audience couldn't broadcast it. It was 1941. The memory of the massacre nine years prior was still in sight. Terror hid and rewrote details about everything, including the discovery. A clumsy crew of men had found the bones by mistake as they sought to uproot and flatten the land on which a railroad would be built. It was a stroke of luck, though the public would never know. Pipil and Lenca workers from the closest coffee plantation unearthed and cleaned the bones. It hurt to know that the bones were familiar—family to some—as they refashioned them to resemble a monster's body. They loaded them on the truck, and then returned to their jobs, invisible once more.

The journalist who failed to ask the important questions nursed his guilt by writing down what he heard whispered on the street. He went as far as sketching out a dinosaur's skeleton on a piece of notebook paper. In place of the dinosaur's skull, he drew in a caricature of President Maximiliano Hernández Martínez, so that a human head sat on the dinosaur's bony neck. The caption read: "Too bad the name *Tyrannosaurus rex* was already taken. Tyrant Lizard King sounds just about right." To destroy the evidence, he lit the pages on fire, leaving only a small gray streak on his desk.

This is what nations are built on, the journalist thought. The belief that we can bury our monstrosities underneath a pile of ash and bones.

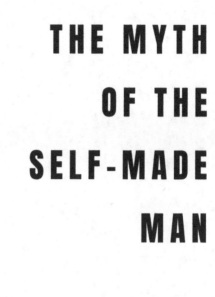

THE MYTH
OF THE
SELF-MADE
MAN

T HE PRESIDENT SMILES DOWN AS VICTOR enters the main atrium, leaving behind the muggy glow of the mid-July sun. The portrait, posed in front of an American flag, hangs above the man working the information desk. Victor approaches, putting on his most professional grin.

As he pivots toward the room for first-time visitors, he drops the façade. He enters his information into a computer—name, birth date, citizenship, institutional affiliation—and poses for a headshot. An employee photocopies his driver's license and asks him to take a seat, where Victor waits for a few minutes. The employee finally hands Victor his research card, its background a grainy version of the Declaration of Independence. The expiration date is a year from today: July 16, 2175.

The card is flimsy, but powerful. A guard swipes it, and Victor pushes past the turnstile into the National Archives' main research room. The sun shines through a floor-to-ceiling glass wall onto groups of people hunched over flat gray tables. Folders lie splayed open in front of them. Victor studies a group to his right and, based on their ages and genders, decides that they must be a tenured faculty member and a couple of research assistants. Their chatter is cordial and light, as if they were at a picnic. Predictably, they're all white.

Victor's goes over rules in his head: Documents can be photographed, but camera bags must be left in the lockers. Looseleaf notes and pencils only. No pens. He hands an archivist the catalog numbers of the boxes he wants and takes a seat at one of the empty tables. They'll bring out his boxes on a cart, which could take anywhere from fifteen minutes to an hour. Victor's adviser warned him about the wait times, but the idle minutes irritate him anyway. He tries to shake the feeling away and refocus on his goal.

He's here to find the Self-Made Man.

If the other researchers are as restless as he is, they don't show it. Could they, like so much of his cohort, have little but vanity riding on their projects? For six years, Victor has poured energy into collecting secondary material related to his area of study: mid–twenty-first century Central American migration to the United States. The digital archives aren't going to be enough to finish his looming, spiraling dissertation, so he's come to excavate the missing pieces of his research. Unlike his classmates, he doesn't have a trust fund to keep him afloat. The academic job market is a sinking ship, but a solid dissertation could be a lifeboat. Or a life preserver, at the very least.

Victor wipes his sweaty palms on his chinos. Unwelcome feelings of inferiority—of being totally out of his depth—creep close, but he scares them away with the memory of what propelled him onto this path. He was an undergraduate, brainstorming topics for a final paper, when he came across an audio clip online. It was a conversation between a cyborg and his owner, and though it was only a few seconds long, Victor listened to it over and over. It was nothing like reading Kant or Heidegger. It was real, urgent, important.

The passage of time threatens to swallow Felipe whole, so Victor has been searching for him ever since.

Where are you from?

I was manufactured in a factory just outside Lewiston, Maine. I grew up in East Boston, from age ten. I went to school in New Haven. And

then I came home, here, when you purchased me
on December eleventh of last year.

But before that, where are you from?

I don't understand your question.

What country are you from?

I was made in America, sir.

*No, that's not what I mean, Felipe. I mean, what country
were you born in? Where did you live before you were
made into a cyborg?*

— —

Felipe.

Sir, my operating system does not seem to have
that information logged.

I told you not to call me sir. I'm your friend, Felipe.

I'm sorry. I don't have an answer to your
question. I was made in America.

The quiet jangle of a cart's wheels interrupts Victor's memories. The government employee pushing it says nothing from
across the room, but Victor knows she's bringing his documents.

"Open one box at a time and look through each folder sep-
arately," the woman instructs. "Handle everything with care."

Much has been written about the mechanics of the Self-Made Man. Victor's read it all. He can recite its basic parts: a network of aluminum-reinforced joints, copper circuitry in its arms and legs, the concealed control panel under the clavicle, a quantum-powered computer in the brain. What's missing from the historical record is the voices of the cyborgs. Historians concerned with the political and economic factors that made the technology so popular overlook the perspectives of the Self-Made Men themselves. Including their voices is a moral and intellectual priority. Hearing Felipe's voice again (or even seeing his face!) would be the breakthrough Victor has been dreaming of.

He's chosen a desk with a bulky monitor because he knows that at least one of the boxes contains DVDs related to the human rights issue he's researching. The cart holds visual materials that the U.S. government chose to keep, mostly instructional guides and advertisements, though many are uncategorized.

The DVDs look nearly identical. Victor flips them over in their plastic sleeves, and they glimmer like disco balls. Touching a finger to his tragus, he syncs his implanted headphones to the computer. Cross-referencing his notes, he checks to make sure he's grabbing a disk from the right decade. He inserts it into the disk drive.

The screen bubbles to life, and a figure in a suit appears. He looks a bit like Victor's brother. Or their father in his youth. The video is paused, so the man remains frozen. Victor squints, searching for an indent on his chest or wiring along his veins. He appears human, though he's disconcertingly handsome. He must be an actor.

He was hoping to find a cyborg, and the fact that the man on-screen isn't one disappoints. But as the disk begins to play, Victor holds his breath. He listens.

Now that you've purchased the Self-Made Man—a best-selling product at Brookstone and the most popular As Seen on TV item of the year—you may be impatiently awaiting the moment you'll be able to flip the power button and get him running. And you should be excited! Our latest cyborg is designed to do everything but disappoint.

The Self-Made Man is made in America, of course. He was assembled in one of our factories, all based in the United States and providing jobs to hundreds of hardworking blue-collar Americans. The composite parts are brought together in one of our fifty factories, and each piece is subjected to thorough quality control. We at Díaz Manufacturing have stuck by our promise to keep assembly and production of every fleet of Self-Made Men local, never exporting labor abroad. Automation has no role in this process. A human runs every diagnostic. Our factories have given a second life to manufacturing towns from Maine to Massachusetts.

Every Self-Made Man is assembled before the base has turned eighteen. Construction at a young age guarantees that the source bodies are malleable enough for the operation that inserts mechanical and electric technologies into their bodies. Then the cyborgs are released into society, where the Self-Made Man works his way up the social ladder.

Before turning eighteen, he's housed in low-income neighborhoods by families who receive generous monthly stipends from Díaz Manufacturing. Living in poverty, on dangerous streets where police helicopters frequent the skies overhead, the Self-Made Man learns hard work, grit, and self-reliance. Then he's sent off to special cyborg-rearing institutions at our partner universities, including Harvard, Stanford, Yale, and Northwestern, to hone his interpersonal skills. After a year working as an assistant in one of our preapproved fields of work—consulting, software engineering, finance, advertising, medicine, or law—the Self-Made Man is put on the market for sale.

At this point, they've been finely tuned, lost any lingering cultural backwardness, and acquired the skills and composure needed to best serve you, the users. Their sensitivity and exposure to our world ensures they'll bring a human touch to their machinelike efficiency. The Self-Made Man is an appliance like no other: He can nanny your newborns or teach you and your family Spanish. He can walk the dog, drive your wife to the doctor, or fill in for you at a parent-teacher conference. Users are discovering new benefits every single day, and our manufacturing and rearing processes ensure he'll assist you with grace, precision, and humility as soon as he powers up.

The Self-Made Man anticipates and responds to your every need, but you can customize his approach through his control panel. If you'd like him to clean your apartment and don't really care how it gets spotless and gleaming, you can simply set his Agency Meter to High Agency. If you're the kind of homeowner who appreciates specificity, simply turn the meter to Low Agency and offer a more detailed set of demands: do the dishes, deep-scrub the kitchen floor, clean the bathrooms, dust the living room, and tidy the bedrooms last.

When this video concludes, the Self-Made Man you ordered will arrive at your doorstep. He'll be holding an envelope with a tablet inside. Open it, and you'll

be able to either textually read or holographically ex-
perience the life trajectory of your individualized Self-
Made Man. As a default, all our devices are named
Cesar, after Cesar Chavez, but you're welcome to
change his name to whatever you'd like.

Any additional questions or concerns can be di-
rected to our customer service line. Thank you for your
purchase and support.

¡La lucha hacia el sueño americano continúa!

The footage is mildly interesting, but it's doesn't offer new information. Victor moves on to the next box, then another. The sun drops, giving the research room a softer glow. Before he knows it, the sky has settled into a blend of pinks and oranges like the soapy, fragrant baths Victor draws for himself after a long day of teaching and classes. The building closes in an hour, but Victor's only gotten through about half the boxes of materials. He wishes he worked faster. If he can't even do archival work well, he might as well drop out of his Ph.D. program. Still, the semester doesn't start until September. He can afford himself some kindness.

Months-long summer breaks are one of Victor's favorite things about being an academic, though he can't escape the blanket of guilt that falls over him when he stops to think about what a privilege they are. There's always work to do: books to read, dissertation chapters to outline, syllabi to draft and edit for classes he'll teach in the fall. But little feels backbreaking or urgent. Sometimes, when he lounges around his Cambridge apartment in nothing but his boxers, Victor remembers the long hours his parents used to work, year-round. His father would take a day off from his office job simply to take Victor and his brother to Raging Waters, a water park just a few miles from their home. His mother would only join if she could wrangle a day of paid leave.

His parents were born after household cyborg use fell out of fashion, but they both had stories of their great-grandparents losing work when the first models hit the market. Recent immigrants who were let go by most of their employers, they disdained the corporations who manufactured cyborgs. Corporate greed ensured their children, and their children's children, struggled for decades.

Victor's life unfolded in the shadow of this anger, shaped by the family lore: Self-Made Men weren't as compassionate or deserving as human workers. Their owners were soulless, motivated solely by efficiency and a marketing budget. Felipe, and an owner who cared enough to figure out where he'd come from, complicated what he'd been taught growing up. Every hour spent in the archive brings Victor a step closer to unearthing the truth of his ancestor's anger: where it came from, whether it was justified, and how knowing his own history might empower him to reshape his future.

The fluorescent lights give the room an unnatural, aseptic feel. With the time he has left, Victor throws a wide net, searching for slivers of evidence, hoping some greater truth will coalesce. He reaches for another box, this one full of magazine and newspaper clippings. He reads the first article, losing himself in the faded ink. What a privilege it is, he thinks, to reconstruct the past.

May 27, 2024
LOS ANGELES, CA—Walterio Díaz's home sits in the Hollywood Hills, in a picturesque neighborhood that overlooks the rest of the city. His property feels like a movie set, with a glistening pool in the backyard pulled straight out of a David Hockney painting. But upon closer inspection, one sees the details that

separate Díaz's multimillion-dollar property from its neighbors: the ceramic sugar skull on his coffee table, a signed photograph of civil rights leader Dolores Huerta, the kitchen's bright collection of small alebrijes, Mexican folk statues of mythical creatures.

Walterio Díaz was born in California's Central Valley to parents who made their living picking strawberries and other fruits, depending on the season.

"My family didn't have much growing up, and when both my parents passed away during my junior year at Princeton, they were in debt. My childhood home went to the bank, and I was forced to stay on campus that summer working to support myself. But all of that gave me the resilience to continue with my studies and to work hard to make something out of myself in this country, a country my parents loved so deeply."

After graduating from Harvard Business School, Díaz worked at the venture capitalist firm Horace Lerner before founding Díaz Manufacturing. The company skyrocketed when they invented the product that brought them international fame: the Self-Made Man. The concept behind it is simple: a male cyborg capable of joining any American family and completing complex tasks that an unfeeling automaton never could.

In an industry that still struggles to represent the nation's demographics, Díaz stands out as one of a handful of Hispanic business moguls. But he says his flagship product is imbued with the same Latino grit and resilience that has shaped his own career.

"My whole life I've had to combat racism and xenophobia," he says candidly. "At Princeton, at

Harvard. You know, at one point someone told me I should make our cyborgs white so that more people would buy them. And you know what I told him? I said, 'Listen, soon we'll be so well-known and our product so popular that white people will be clearing out our shelves. They're not going to care about the color of his skin once they see what the Self-Made Man can do.'"

Díaz is dedicated to uplifting individuals who come from backgrounds like his. His company's website boasts that more than 50 percent of employees at Díaz Manufacturing are Hispanic, including many in upper management. Every year at Princeton, Díaz personally funds twenty tuition scholarships earmarked for undergraduate students with Latin American heritage.

"I try helping my community, *mi pueblo*, however I can," he says. "That's one of the reasons I'm proud that the Self-Made Man is so popular. This country has a long history of xenophobia and hatred toward immigrants, but I hope that our product is showing Americans all the beautiful things about our people. It proves we are hardworking people, helpful to this country and its economy."

When asked if he has any lingering thoughts he'd like to share, Walterio Díaz pauses. His answer is succinct and sounds like it's been used many times before. Yet as he speaks, it feels genuine. "This country has given me my American dream. I just want to help others achieve theirs."

September 4, 2029
NEW YORK, NY—A hotly anticipated documentary

outlining over three decades of labor malpractices in the cyborg industry arrives on Netflix today. *No Land of Our Own: A Look Inside America's Automated-Help Industry* follows employees at a factory in Maine, who claim that Díaz Manufacturing constantly underpaid unionized workers, hired undocumented migrants, and knowingly maintained substandard working conditions.

The film premiered earlier this year at Sundance, sparking an ongoing investigation by the U.S. Department of Labor. A spokesperson for Díaz Manufacturing denied allegations of twelve-hour workdays and workplace intimidation in an e-mailed statement to the *Times*. "In addition to the fabrications and exaggerations that run throughout the reporting, the documentary selectively edits the clips to produce a convenient narrative. Díaz Manufacturing was founded by the son of Mexican farmworkers and fair labor practices have been central to the company's mission since its inception."

Filmmakers Dan Kaine and Janice Twill stand by their documentary, which they say points out the hypocrisy of the product that made Díaz a multibillionaire. "The Self-Made Man has long been paraded as a way of making Americans' lives easier. Hell, we were considering purchasing one ourselves, before we started this project. But the fact that this CEO abuses thousands of workers while claiming to take the burden off his customers? That sort of hypocrisy needs to be called out."

Available to stream now, *No Land of Our Own* will also have a limited theatrical release in October.

February 4, 2030

WASHINGTON, D.C.—Early this afternoon, Congress passed a bill that would require cyborg manufacturing companies to disclose the use of imported machinery in their products. In a rare show of bipartisanship, lawmakers from both parties say the bill will support cyborg production in the United States and prevent the outsourcing of manufacturing jobs abroad.

"The economy is struggling, unemployment is up, and Americans are losing their jobs to people working in India and Honduras," Brad Floyd, junior senator from Maine, wrote in a press release shortly after the Senate vote. "There are jobs for people in manufacturing all over the world, except right here in their own communities. This bill ensures that America comes first, and that American companies make jobs for more Americans on American soil. It's that simple."

Floyd first introduced the bill with Democratic Senator Armando Flores of California a year ago. Just a few weeks earlier, the *Times* reported that the cyborg production company Díaz Manufacturing was importing components used in its flagship product, the Self-Made Man. The company marketed and tagged all its products as made in America. The parts were assembled in factories in Maine, but metal cylinders used in the body, as well as the control box connected to the base's central nervous system, were all made in El Salvador. Internal leaks brought the issue to Senator Floyd's attention, prompting the bill.

CEOs of the most prominent cyborg companies in the country criticized the bill and urged the president to veto it. "Our companies are all based in the United States," a joint statement reads. "We create thousands and thousands of jobs every year, stimulating the economy when it most needs it. These regulations should be considered unconstitutionally high tariffs. They're going to make it fiscally impossible to continue what we've been doing: creating jobs and products that make life easier for average Americans."

Victor scribbles down the name. *Walterio Díaz*. It sounds familiar, as if he culled it from a jargon-filled article but quickly lost it among his subconscious clutter. Either way, it's not an artifact from Felipe's life. The instructional guide and newspaper clips might corroborate secondary reading, but they don't tell him anything about Felipe. Did have his own bedroom? What did he eat every morning? Oatmeal? Or was cooking a new breakfast each morning a way to stave off boredom?

Days pass in a frustrating cycle: Metro, research room, frustration, hotel room, loneliness, cable television, despair. A handful of acquaintances live in D.C., but instead of texting them, Victor spends nights half watching terrible action movies. Three days before he's set to leave D.C., he still hasn't found a trace of Felipe.

Desperation lands Victor outside the archivist's office. He pauses at the door. Logically, asking for help is easy. The person sitting behind the door—probably old, probably white—is paid to know the archive's every crevice. They field dozens of questions a day, a handful of them surely less interesting or worthwhile than Victor's, but still, he struggles to reach for the handle. Asking for help feels like admitting his faults, proof that he keeps barging into rooms with no space for someone like him. He thinks of the professor and his assistants. Would they hesitate? Would they turn away? Victor steps through.

The archivist sits behind a desk. Victor explains his project and that he's seeking primary documents related to mid-century cyborgs.

"Any medium?" the archivist asks.

"Anything from the perspective of a Self-Made Man."

"Sometimes we catalog by topic, usually when the Smithsonian is looking for materials for an exhibit." He types into his computer and leans in slightly, squinting. "A couple years back we compiled materials on asylum policy. Some of the materials are from far before the time period you're looking at, but there might be something good."

The archivist scribbles on a sticky note and hands it over. The interaction is painless. Victor thanks the man, who lazily waves him off. After another bout of waiting, the cart hobbles toward him. The boxes seem identical to the ones he's combed through already, though there are fewer of them. He again reaches for the closest box. The label on the side reads: TESTIMONIOS. He wonders why it's labeled in Spanish.

The clip plays on the monitor. The opening seconds of static give way to an almost-recognizable background: a banner with indecipherable print, a wooden altar, portraits of Jesus and Mary peppering the back wall. The camera zooms in on a man standing at the front of a meeting hall. He's young, no older than twenty-five. His tan skin is leathered, a sign of long days under the sun. Before he's said anything, he runs a hand through his hair and Victor makes out lines of metal wiring where his veins should run. Then he notices that his eyelids move like a camera's shutter. The Self-Made Man opens his mouth. He speaks.

Let me tell you about my kidnapping.
You'll have to forgive me, for many of the details
are blurry. I was young when it happened, and I have

*more than a suspicion that my memories were tam-
pered with in that refurbished textile factory in Maine.
There are gaps I'll never be able to fill, scenes I'll never
be able to fully re-create. But I can promise you that
my pain, the traumatic life I have lived, is real. I feel it
on my body, on my soft flesh, and even in my rewired
cyborg brain.*

When I was an eight-year-old boy, I left my home
in Coatepeque, a town in El Salvador that sits on the
edge of a lake. My town was lively, and my parents
supported me for much of my life with their restaurant. I worked taking orders and bringing out dishes
to the patrons, and though business wavered during
the winter months, our busy summers made up for it.
During the warmer months, people from San Salvador
and other parts of the country loved coming to swim,
sunbathe, eat mariscos, and drink pilsners.

But soon people stopped coming. You see, our little town was overrun by a series of small plagues that
kept people away. I'm not certain which was the worst,
and I don't think we can point to one particular curse
that ruined our lives. That's not the important part. It
doesn't matter whether people left because the lakeside
properties were flooding, because gangs had moved in,
or because the economy had tanked and they didn't
have money to spend.

What matters is that we became very poor, very
quickly. We had to close the restaurant, and I'd fall
asleep hallucinating because my stomach was eating
itself. In my dreams, I'd be visited by a blond woman
carrying a basket of bread and fruits, and I could tell
that she was beautiful even though I could never see
her face. But every time I'd reach out to grab a piece of

food, I'd wake up shaking and clutching my stomach.

Many boys my age had already left for the United States, and by the time I packed my own bag with just one change of clothes, I'd heard about how terrifying the journey was. Mami warned me. She said, "Mijo, boys like you get robbed, raped, detained by Mexican policemen. They fall off the top of freight trains that take them through the countryside, their bodies are left unmarked and unclaimed on the tracks, they're killed by gang members, they get ill and die. Boys die every day, mijo."

But I was running out of options, and if I made it—on the off chance I made it—I might find a job and send money back to my family. There were no guarantees, but there was the possibility that their stomachs wouldn't hurt so much, and maybe they'd be able to return to their lives as they'd known them. To give them a shot at a dignified life, I swallowed my fear and made the trip knowing well that it could cost me my life.

Forgive my tears. I feel weak when I cry, but I can't help it. Remembering what I've gone through is difficult. My brothers always called me a chillón for crying so often when I was a child, so I forced myself to make my face an unmoving stone, like one of those Mayan sculptures they display in museums in this country. When I cry now, it's like a pipe bursting. When I speak about my past—a series of events I do not have full recollection of—it's as if someone outside of myself has flipped a switch, releasing all my emotions.

Crossing the border from El Salvador into Guatemala was in some ways the easiest part of the trip. You don't need a visa or anything. You just show your passport, and the customs people let you enter the country. If it's a large group, those, what-do-you-call-'em, caravans. The American politicians call them caravans. If it's a caravan, the policemen at the border could get a little more aggressive, but it's usually nothing extreme.

But in other ways, the Guatemala–El Salvador border was one of the toughest stops in my exile. I don't mean that it was the most violent part. My bruises and torn skin, arms looking as if they'd been put through a cheese grater—those I got in Mexico and the United States. But when I entered Guatemala, I felt an earthquake through my inner self. As I looked out the window of the bus I'd ridden all the way from San Salvador, I knew I was looking over the land I was born in for the last time. Don't ask me how I knew that for certain, but I did.

I didn't know that this would be my fate—that I'd look like this, that I'd have metal in my veins—but I knew I wouldn't be one of the Salvadoreños who return. Members of my family often have dreams, visions, and premonitions. This was the first time I'd had one, but it has proven correct so far.

As I watched El Salvador disappear over the horizon, I tried to remember every detail. Don't get me wrong, much of Guatemala looks and feels like El Salvador does. The heat is the same, the plants are too. Borders don't define much. But the heartbreak was palpable. It was a debilitating misery. Combined with the hunger I felt after nearly two days without a bite to eat, I almost stayed on that bus, not caring where it'd take me next. Somehow, though, I managed to pull my aching body off the seat. I was directed by a coyote who'd been paid to guide a group of about twenty of us, though most were Guatemalans who'd just begun their journey. I had already deserted my homeland, my body and mind deteriorating in the process.

Here is where my memories begin to get fuzzy, where the gaps widen and the silence grows. The people who took me in after I escaped, those who brought me here to speak with you, they tell me that my memory falters because of how my brain was hardwired to make me a more loyal helper. All I have is snapshots, like the fear of hanging off the edge of a freight train, the pain of getting slashed by another migrant for the meager bits of cash I carried, and the harassment by policemen, the worst of which I'm grateful to have forgotten. If God has given me one gift among all my turmoil, it's the loss of details, though the pain remains real.

Somehow, I made it to the border. The one you know. The one from the news. The U.S.-Mexico border. The coyote spotted a white truck in the distance and ran, leaving the rest of us scrambling. I took shelter between a couple of shrubs, and just when I figured it was safe to emerge, a pair of strong hands grasped my dirty, sweat-stained T-shirt. The man wore black leather gloves in the hot Sonoran sun. I wondered how he could bear the heat. His hands must have sweated as he gripped my throat, pressing down until I was kneeling, the sand burning my bare knees. My jeans had ripped somewhere near Guadalajara, so I'd cut them into shorts. Dark fists thundered down on my temples. I attempted to fight back, but I was only a boy at the time, and there was no way I was going to overpower a full-grown man. My kidnapper towered over me, hitting me over and over until I passed out.

I woke up under the high roof of a warehouse, encaged in four walls of chain-link fencing. Half a dozen other boys lay next to me. Some were crying, others were yelling, and many, like me, sat in a scared silence. Through the fencing, I could see other cages and dozens of other boys. They had separated us, but we could see the terror painting each other's faces.

A few of the other boys in my enclosure were also from El Salvador. Others were from neighboring nations on my little slice of the continent: Honduras, Guatemala, Nicaragua. There were a few Haitians and African immigrants who'd made their way to Tijuana and then tried their luck at the border. A common fate connected us, whether we spoke Creole or our own regional Spanish dialects. We'd been kidnapped, we were caged, and we were about to be sold to Americans in plain sight.

Against my will, without my consent, I had my body and mind taken from me. I was sedated with small doses of drugs snuck into my food. While I was unconscious, I went through a dozen different surgeries that reinforced my joints with metal hinges, installed small wires that now run parallel to my tendons, and replaced pieces of me with various pieces of machinery. My neurosurgery was the last modification, and by that point the anesthetics had begun to wear out. They inserted a computer in my brain and wiped out hundreds of hours of my own memories, putting software in their place. It was like a hot knife in my skull. I have a headache just thinking of it now. Soon after, I lost consciousness again.

When I awoke, I was in a house I didn't recognize. It was spotless. Paintings and smiling family portraits stared at me from the walls. I met my new family, my *owners. They assigned me tasks, and though I had no desire to complete them, my limbs obeyed. I took out the trash, landscaped the backyard, assembled furniture, walked the children to school. After just a couple of months, my back hurt. I was accused of stealing even though my own instruction manual says I am programmed to be physically incapable of theft.*

Americans say that Self-Made Men enjoy the work, that we comply because we have no sense of ourselves before we were manufactured. They point to how willingly we help and how we even seem to love the families we work for. That's mechanics, not anatomy. I was condemned to follow their bidding, and though the settings on my emotional meter released a flow of endorphins to my body, anger simmered inside my body too. I wouldn't understand the scope of my imprisonment until I met the wonderful volunteers at Southside Presbyterian, but even then, as I lived it, my body yearned for freedom.

After years of suffering, I escaped by sheer chance. There's a glitch in the technology used to hardwire the brains of Self-Made Men. It appears after several years. If our Agency Meter is turned to the highest setting, it gives us more autonomy than the manufacturers intended. The eldest child in the family, a ten-year-old named Sarah, was toying with my settings. I'm unsure what she was trying to do, but she left my Agency Meter at the highest possible setting. Then, when no one was home, I escaped through a gate in the backyard and never looked back.

After I ran away and the organization who brought me here tonight offered me sanctuary, I learned what had happened to me and those other boys. We were kidnapped by men working for a company called Díaz Manufacturing. They gather hundreds of children at the border every year, and load them, unconscious, into trucks that bring them to warehouses thousands of miles away. The company keeps saying that the boys they source are lab-grown, or otherwise ethically acquired, but I'm here to prove that they've been lying. I never asked to be this way. I never asked to be a Self-Made Man.

Violence, in both minuscule and enormous forms, takes its toll. As I stand in front of you in this church, know that I've only been able to reconstruct the story I'm telling tonight with a lot of help, with a lot of therapy, and with hours of deep digging. And I know that my narrative, the one I've tried to lay out as faithfully and succinctly as possible, is not unique. All those other boys in captivity? All sold. The hundreds of thousands that came before and after me? You can find them in almost every suburb in this country.

I'm asking that you, as lovers of freedom and justice and as Americans, help us right this wrong. Children don't deserve to be kidnapped and kept away from their families any longer. This is happening under our noses, but it persists because we don't care. We listen to the company's spokespeople when they tell us nothing is amiss, that their product is only meant to help us. And because it is convenient, we believe the talking heads and we ignore the children at the border.

The pamphlets you received when you walked in tonight have more detailed steps on how to help: boycotting Díaz Manufacturing, donating to our organization, raising awareness about this kidnapping crisis. Perhaps the most important thing you can do, though, *is to help people like me—refugees, men stripped of their freedom—retrieve some of our humanity.*

This country, this company, has stripped me of so much—not least of all my name. My owners called me Pedro. My name is José Manuel Hernandez. This is my story. Listen to it, I beg you. Listen to my people when we tell you who we are and why we're here. Listen to them so I can leave this chapel and finally live out in the open, free of fear or persecution. Like the Bible says in John 8:32, "And you shall know the truth, and the truth shall make you free."

I've told you the truth, and now I ask that you help me in our struggle toward liberation. Stand with me until we are all free.

Several months later, in Cambridge, Victor stares out at the soft flurry of snow that makes February feel gentler than it is. He opens the folder on his computer with his archival documents. It's a portal to the past, and he immediately returns to the research room, the place where he saw José Manuel Hernandez for the first time.

The clip ended, and a scream swelled in Victor's gut. He bit his tongue and restarted the video. Immediately after it ended, he hit play again. For rest of the afternoon, he drowned himself in José's voice. His anxieties quieted. His dissertation, Felipe, his loneliness, his job prospects, the burden of racial capitalism—they all became faint whispers under the sound of José's confession.

Victor has no idea what happened to José after he spoke in that church. Did he stay in the United States, or did he return to El Salvador? There were a set of experimental, often deadly, procedures used to try making cyborgs fully human again. Did José participate? Victor doesn't know, and probably never will. The past is an ever-growing cavern, and even a lifetime of spelunking won't reveal it all. After the trip to the National Archives, Victor put the project away for several weeks. Listening to José's story over and over again exhausted him.

His dissertation is almost complete, but by his own account, he's failed. When he set off on this project more than eight years ago, he wanted to pull together a biography of Felipe, the Self-Made Man. It'd be an interrogation of history through the eyes of the most dispossessed. And perhaps most importantly, he'd be the one to pull him from the archive, to save him from oblivion. He'd make a name for himself by honoring the Self-Made Man's.

Nothing new has surfaced in all these years of research. History will swallow nearly everything Felipe went through. Victor has failed.

Still, his adviser is optimistic. A comparative approach fits better into what his department has asked for, and it's allowed him to engage with theory: human/nonhuman lines as borders, childhood as a sociohistorical construction, fallacies of historical positivism. He's been able to fold José's testimony into some secondary readings, cobbling together a composite portrait of a Self-Made Man. It's not what Victor imagined for himself, but he's coming to accept the gap between expectation and reality.

Tens of thousands of words unfurl before him in neat lines. If he puts in the work during the weeks before his defense, he might be able to eke out a departmental award. That could lead to a teaching appointment, and then a book, and maybe someday a tenure-track position. He might find a semblance of stability in a notoriously unstable ivory tower. Victor types away as the snow sticks to the window and melts, the warmth inside emanating through the glass.

And then, as he nears the end of his two hours of daily writing time, he gets an email from a National Archives staff member. There is no subject line, and the body is terse.

Victor,
> Freedom of Information Act (FOIA) lawsuit against the Dept. of Labor declassified new asylum materials. Perhaps of interest.

Attached are scans of three department memos and an audio clip. Victor feels a ringing in his ears. He opens the MP3 file and hits play.

What was your name? Before I gave you one. Before I named you Felipe.

——

What was your name, Felipe?

My operating system doesn't seem to have that information logged.

Felipe—

But . . .

Yes?

If you turn my agency settings up, I may be able to remember.

There. It's done.

Give me a second.

— —

— —

— —

Felipe.

I'm trying. I'm trying to remember. I'm trying to construct something out of the gaps.

Keep trying. What was your name?

— —

— —

— —

When my mother needed to get my attention, she'd yell out from the doorway of our adobe home. Chuy, she'd yell. Chuy, come help me with the plates. Chuy, go help your uncle bring the cows back from the plot of land. Chuy, stop playing with that fucking dog and come help me.

Your name was Chuy?

My name is Chuy. Jesus Alejandro Guzmán Rivera.

I'm changing that right now in your interface. I'm changing your name from Felipe to Chuy. I am so sorry; I had no idea you had a name until I saw on the news . . . until I saw a man like you on the television.

When I had a family, they called me Chuy. I'm

from El Salvador, and I used to have a family.
I'm a Self-Made Man, and my name is Jesus
Alejandro Guzmán Rivera.

*Chuy, is there anything I could do to make your life
easier? To make your stay with us more comfortable?
We want you to feel part of the family.*

You could let me go.

What?

You could free me. You could leave my agency
settings at this level and let me walk out that
door. I've been reading the news too. There are
organizations that help people like me. I just
need to be released from my duties here.

*Felipe. Chuy. I can't do that. You know I can't do that for
you. We love you, Chuy.*

You're right. I'm sorry I asked. Here I have a bed
and food and television. Yes, my hands hurt from
all the yard work I've been doing lately, and my
calluses have split open. But I am happy to be
here. I think the adjustment of my agency settings
has interfered with my brain's processors. You
should change it back. I don't think I want to be
freed at all. I don't even know why I asked.

*Maria is going to be so excited to know your new
name, and to know where you're from. Her parents are
from Latin America too. Her mother is from Mexico and*

her father was born in Argentina. I mean, we bought you because we were supporting a Hispanic-owned business. We could have bought one of those white men—"born into greatness," "of the most supreme quality," or whatever their product's slogan is—but no. We wanted you.

Ah yes. She's mentioned that before. Supporting a Chicano company. Just what her mother would have wanted. Yes, sir.

Oh, I'm so happy to know your name, Chuy. I'm so, so happy to have such a wonderful Self-Made Man in our home.

The audio clip is short, and there is so much left unsaid. Victor could slip Felipe's real name into the dissertation, perhaps to reiterate a point he's already made or as a stowaway footnote, but it won't dictate its success or failure. And, though it hurts to admit, writing the name down might not actually save it from the passage of time. To be found, someone must care enough to search.

Instead, Victor scribbles down the name in the Moleskin notebook at the edge of his desk. He shuts his laptop. History might forget the Self-Made Man, but he won't. He'll hold the new name close, right beside his own.

QUIERO
PERREAR!
AND OTHER
CATASTROPHES

As MANUEL CISNEROS AWOKE ONE MORNING from uneasy dreams, he found himself transformed in bed into a gigantic reggaeton star.

He stumbled to the bathroom, where he noticed a tattoo on his neck. A black and red serpent coiled downward, its head resting on his clavicle. All over his body, unexpected gradients of colored ink bloomed like an allergic reaction: a spattering of stars near his wrist, a Puerto Rican flag on his right bicep, a Dominican one on his left, the names of women in cursive on his forearm, the crest from the Salvadoran flag on his right calf. They were his tattoos, Manuel knew, but the needles piercing his skin felt like delusions pulled from a deep slumber.

Manuel could recite the facts of his life. He had a career as a reggaetonero; a certified star at only twenty-three. The tattoos had cost a couple grand each, but he could afford them easily. The details, though, were hazy. Dreams, not memories. How had he accrued all the fame, all the money? A dizziness set in, as if he'd stood up too quickly.

A phone call interrupted his thoughts, and before the vertigo had subsided, he'd been corralled into the back of a silver Cadillac.

"When you play Staples Center next weekend," Manuel's manager said as they zigzagged down Santa Monica Boulevard, "we want to make sure it's memorable. The Wilbur, the House of Blues, the Observatory? Those were nice venues, sure. Yeah. But this is the big leagues. We need to make it spectacular. Daddy Yankee–level shit."

He pulled a laptop from underneath the seat.

"Here's the final cut of the video that'll play right before you go on. Get the hype going, remind the fans why they love you."

The black screen opened to an aerial view of Los Angeles. Manuel recognized the song as his own but couldn't recall the title. The beat picked up, instrumentals came in, and his stage name, Manu-C, popped on-screen. Vocals layered on: low, sensual, rhythmic. It was his voice. Manuel moved his lips loosely, reading the lyrics on-screen. Chains hung off his neck, gold peeked out from his teeth. Every inch of himself was supersize. The man on-screen danced in a way Manuel knew he wasn't capable of, as if he were watching a body double. The song wasn't terrible, but Manuel wondered why it wasn't angstier, a bit less produced. Briefly, he remembered growing up on Arctic Monkeys and the Smiths. Or was it Kaiser Chiefs and the Strokes? He kept second-guessing himself.

"Where are we going?" Manuel said in an unsuccessful attempt to shake off the fogginess.

"Coño! I told you last night. We have a meeting with Celeste's team," his manager said. He didn't know a Celeste, but Manuel nodded.

The label's offices were an open workspace flanked by glass-walled offices. A suit typed away furiously at his desktop. Another held a landline phone to his ear, forehead creased. And in the main conference room, a woman. A beautiful young woman, probably around Manuel's age.

Celeste was gorgeous. Stunning, really. Her face soft, her chin and jaw rounded out in a way that complemented her cheekbones, accentuated by a carefully applied layer of highlight. Her eye shadow was done in bright shades of pink, an ombré that became lighter the farther it got from her eyelids. She had a sleeve of tattoos up her left arm, all much more tasteful than Manuel's. Celeste wore baggy cargo pants and a spaghetti-strapped top, a combination fashionable in the moment precisely because it recalled another decade. Her complexion was even; a smooth, glistening brown.

He wondered if this was why he'd woken up like this, if the absurd, disorienting morning he'd floated through was supposed to bring him to her.

Earlier that day—just after daybreak, on the other side of town—Celeste awoke unchanged. She was still an artist struggling to really break into the industry, scurrying around town with a handful of singles, but no radio hits. With the nimble fingers of a lifelong pianist, she applied a face of makeup and called a car to the label's offices.

Her manager greeted her with a kiss, his freshly trimmed stubble prickly against her cheek, before launching into a soft pitch yet again.

Manu-C had a problem, and Celeste could be the solution. A tabloid fabricated a rumor claiming the reggaeton superstar was gay. It would have died off quietly, but when a slightly more reputable celebrity magazine brought the question up in an interview, the star fumbled, answering with ambiguity. The rumor blew up, so much so that it got a full segment on Telemundo. His team had a PR crisis on their hands.

Manu-C was easy to find online, in his music videos and on his social media pages, but Celeste was unimpressed. Most of his videos, like those of so many male reggaetoneros, relied on half-naked, light-skinned women splayed across the screen. Somehow, he was both boring and offensive.

"Sure, he doesn't totally align with your brand, but this could be huge for you," her manager said.

Celeste's morals told her to skip the meeting entirely, but her business sense said she should hear Manu-C's team out. Her career path hadn't been breezy or predictable, so the temptation was palpable. She was the Queens-born daughter of Ecuadorian immigrants who'd built a career through a cocktail of favors, luck, and sheer will. Her songs, titled things like "No Que No" and "Como Tú," were marketed for their niche feminist messages. (Celeste's first music video showed her and a girl gang robbing an abusive ex-boyfriend's bodega.) Despite all her small victories, she still hadn't won the luxury to forgo opportunism. The patriarchy was churning its rusty old gears, squeezing Celeste into a position she'd rather not be in.

Then she spotted him through the glass. She'd expected a cocky macho man who walked brutishly, obviously overcompensating. Instead, his eyes flitted around the room restlessly, soaking in as many details as they could, as if newly discovering the office. He was shorter than she'd imagined, and he looked much kinder in person. Without a word, he sat across from her, his pupils on hers for only a second.

"I got nothing against gay people, but this shit hurts our sales," Manu-C's manager said, before diving into the proposal. "It's easy. We let the paparazzi catch you lounging around Los Angeles, and then Manu-C brings you onstage at Staples Center for a collab. The label releases the song first thing in the morning, then announces your album. Our publicists confirm the relationship a few days later."

"Win-win-win." Celeste's manager shrugged. "Celeste becomes even more famous, the rumors stop, and we all make a shit ton of money."

Celeste's eyes landed on Manuel, the handsome but ordinary man across from her. If she kissed him, ran her manicured fingers through his curly hair, and pretended she was enjoying herself, she could cement herself as an artist worth listening to, though she'd surely be relegated to an explanation after a comma: *Manuel Cisnero's latest girlfriend, rising reggaeton artist Celeste*. Once, in middle school, Celeste had read that when anglerfish mate, the male becomes an appendage of the larger female, relying on her for nutrients, for survival. If she said yes, that's who she'd become. Overnight, she could go from reggaeton artist to reggaeton star, from mere mortal to untouchable goddess. There'd be thousands of people on the other side, waiting, listening, longing for her next song. She could run the reggaeton industry, but only if she strapped herself to a man's side. A parasite on the illusion of male genius.

Celeste had kept quiet while the managers went back and forth on logistics. Besides a couple of nods, Manu-C hadn't reacted much. To grab his attention, and to make a career decision before she lost her will, she spoke up.

"Let's do it," she said. Maybe dating a man publicly (even if disingenuously) would complicate her stage persona. A men-ain't-shit feminist in love with a quasi-problematic reggaeton star. What a concept.

Hearing about his life, Manuel's brain flitted from revelation to revelation. He had fans! There was a rumor about him on national news. And then Celeste's face, unforgettable and destined for fame. She had the whole look, unlike he, who, the morning after, still hadn't changed out of his ratty plaid boxers and an oversize tee that read SOMEONE WHO LOVES ME VERY MUCH WENT TO THE DOMINICAN REPUBLIC AND GOT ME THIS T-SHIRT.

He couldn't remember how he'd ended up in this bare and bougie penthouse. Vaguely, he knew there'd been a different house in a different city. A less flashy zip code he'd grown up in. At least he thought so. No time to dwell—he was set to meet Celeste at the Grove in an hour.

"Big man in town," Celeste said when they spotted a poster advertising Man-C's concert plastered to the side of an art deco façade. He tried to smile, but it felt like pulling taffy. If she noticed, she didn't let on. Celeste intertwined her fingers in his and pulled him into one of the luxury storefronts, slowly enough to stay in sight of the gaping camera lens a few feet away.

A security guard trailed them for a couple steps, until he noticed their designer clothes. They shrugged off a salesperson who offered assistance a few seconds later. From shelves and racks, they gently grabbed glittery things they didn't need: teeny handbags, studded heels, snakeskin belts, necklaces, rings, diamond earrings.

"I need to tell you something. Before we go any further . . ." Manuel said.

"We're not having sex, so no need to disclose whatever you have going on down there," Celeste said.

"No, I'm serious."

"Go on, chikibaby," Celeste said. She'd stopped to try on a try on a pair of six-hundred-dollar sunglasses.

"You know how when you wake up, before you shake the feeling, whatever happened in your dreams feels real? The past day or so, I've been stuck living in that limbo. Everything related to my life as a celebrity seems impossible, but I know it's happened."

Celeste looked at him with a blank face.

"My past is hazy," Manuel said. "Details slip. I'm uncertain what's real and what's a mind trick. I can buy whatever I want at this store, but I don't remember making enough money to afford it. It's like I had a brain aneurism or a stroke or something."

"If you're playing a game with me, it's not very fun."

"I wouldn't waste your time like that. I'm here, talking to you. That's real, solid."

Manuel handed his credit card to the cashier, paying for Celeste's sunglasses and a pair of rings for himself. They headed to a lunch reservation, but steps away from the restaurant's front door Celeste turned her body toward him.

"Does this feel like a dream?" she asked, pulling him in for a kiss. Her body was soft against his. He snaked his tongue into her mouth, but when she met it with hers, he pulled back. Not because he was disgusted, but because he hadn't expected her to reciprocate.

"That was very real," Manuel said. Celeste returned his smile before walking inside and ordering them each a glass of prosecco.

"I don't remember any of my songs," he confessed. "I don't know what the hell I'm going to do at Staples Center."

"I'm sure muscle memory will kick in. Your shit is . . . simple enough."

"Ouch." Manuel took a sip of champagne from a crystal flute. Honesty made him feel less crazy, so he kept talking. "I don't know how to dance. I remember almost nothing about reggaeton."

"You're Puerto Rican, aren't you? You have to know something. Wisin & Yandel. Don Omar. Plan B. You know them."

"No."

"Ivy Queen? Ozuna? Arcángel? Zion & Lennox?"

"Nope."

"You're in trouble." Celeste laughed. She could be softening herself to him for the sake of the cameras, but the smile felt organic, more relaxed than when she'd greeted him that morning. As they stood to leave, Manuel pulled Celeste toward his chest, not caring whether a cameraman caught them or not. He planted two kisses on her, the first on the lips and the second on her check.

"You'll help me, then?" Manuel asked. Celeste nodded, turning to stand with her back against his chest.

"We can figure it out before the show." She pulled his hands around her waist and leaned her head back against his shoulder.

"Maybe you'll wake up tomorrow and you'll be your boring old self again."

"God willing," Manuel said. He dug his nose into her neck. Her perfume was warm, floral. When they couldn't force it any longer, they retreated to the car waiting for them.

The man was unmoored from reality by drugs, fame, or some other vice, but he was also extremely handsome. Back in the label's office, Celeste had been preoccupied, but in the afternoon light of the Grove she couldn't deny the features that made him so beloved. Dark skin, blemish-free. A soft layer of scruff covering his jawline. Teeth as straight and shiny as a cartoon character's. For an afternoon, she glimpsed a future where she could indulge — eat anywhere, buy anything — without having to sacrifice or fight for a moment of sweetness. They'd kissed and she didn't hate it.

Still, there was a whole team behind him, and she had no idea if his cluelessness was part of the ploy. She'd found him endearing, but she couldn't let her guard down. Men in the industry often seemed harmless, until they weren't. As the driver shuttled her to rehearsal, she tapped the edges of her bright pink acrylics against the window. If it came down it, she was fairly certain she could claw free.

The dance studio was cold. Manu-C arrived five minutes late but ready to practice. His dancing was terrible — stiffer and clumsier than in clips she'd watched the night before. Limbs flew as Manu-C gave it his all, like he needed to prove his fame was earned, not a fluke.

"Let's take a break," Manuel eventually said. They'd hit their marks, figured out their entrances, and outlined the general movement across the stage, but when it came to the actual perreo, the down-and-dirty, they fizzled. The self-assured sex fiend from the tabloids was nowhere to be found. Manu-C was just a guy, trying his best.

"Okay, okay," Celeste said. "Back to basics. Loosen your shoulders."

Minutes went by.

"Move your hips, not your shoulders."

The track restarted every few seconds. Celeste's vocals complemented his well. The song would be a hit.

"Drop it low, use your thigh muscles."

She coached him, slowly coaxing out the superstar out.

"Get closer to me," she said. Manu-C pressed his body against her until they were both breathing heavy. It'd been a while since she'd had anyone this close, but she didn't mind. He didn't seem to either. Until the music stopped abruptly, she could ignore the artifice and pretend they'd found each other on a random dance floor.

"Not half-bad," he said. "Thank you."

"You seem to be yourself again."

"Not exactly. I'm getting there. Maybe."

He unscrewed a bottle of water and handed it to her. Their fingers grazed each other's but neither reacted. Being with Manu-C was easy, easier than she'd expected. For so long, she'd been taught that success came with sacrifice, and that the easy path yielded little of worth. This felt different, as if it were possible to live a life both enjoyable and profitable.

"Let's run it one more time," she said, offering Manuel her palm. For days, they rehearsed. He got a hold of the perreo, and they perfected it.

Celeste's back arched, and she pressed her ass just below Manuel's waistline. He gripped her side, pulling her in tight, before slinking his pinkie along her hipbone. She grinded on him, and he tried matching her rhythm.

Muffled screams and a bass line reverberated backstage. A round of cheers signaled the end of the opening act.

"You ready?" Celeste asked. Her body stiffened as she stopped perreando.

"I won't move my hips as well as you do, but I'll try my best, chikibaby," Manuel said.

From her seat—front row, just below the stage—Celeste watched the opening number. Lights strobed and spun, illuminating the thousands of fans who packed seats up to the rafters. Manu-C's face filled the giant screens, sparking screams all the way up to the nosebleeds. When he came onstage, he danced with a microphone loosely held up to his lips. He zoomed around the stage singing, quick and effortless. He hadn't had time to learn all his lyrics and would be lip-synching half his set. (Celeste wasn't seeking sainthood.) But he delivered the words from his opening song as if it were the only reason he'd been placed on Earth. His gold jewelry glimmered under the stage lights, and the beads of sweat on his skin shined like pearls.

If his partial amnesia was a boyish gag, he'd sold it well. Short of fully believing him, Celeste had seen how it'd weighed him down, making him clumsy and self-conscious during rehearsals. Now, seeing him come alive onstage, she let herself smile. Los Angeles was a lonely city, and it'd been months since she'd seen how a real connection could untangle even the most jumbled life. The superstar onstage was proof. The spectacle was, in part, her creation.

About halfway through the show, a sensual bass synth melded with the quick beats of a snare drum. The song established a melody line that even the most dedicated fans didn't recognize. It was Celeste's new track. She began to sing. *No creas que te necisito, solo porque chingamos un ratito.* A spotlight found her. It was hot on her skin. She made her way toward Manuel and allowed him to pull her in. She gyrated, and as he entered his verse, he leaned in. She felt him harden against her. Their bodies were slick. Celeste huffed as she caught her breath. When the song ended, they laughed, then kissed. Manuel's lips tasted salty on hers. She stayed there, his arms pulling her close, for a second longer than she needed to.

The hard-on didn't embarrass him. Celeste was beautiful, and there were thousands of people screaming out for him. The bright glare of fans' phone cameras filled the stadium like a swarm of fireflies. The rush of blood—up his neck, down his waist—was unavoidable. When they debuted her new song, the shrieks swelled. Celeste didn't complain. She strutted offstage, leaving him to finish his set alone.

As soon as the show ended, he was ushered backstage and toward his dressing room by a group of bodyguards. This was another part of his life that now felt uncanny. He was seldom alone or fully in charge of his own life. Someone organized pickups and drop-offs. Another person set his schedule. His manager, security, or some other powerful man stood by him whenever he was in public. A faint urge for freedom percolated in the back of his head. Perhaps that's why he reacted to the man shouting out his name as he stepped into his dressing room.

"Wait," he told security. "I know him. Let him through."

The man closed the dressing room door without Manuel asking, smiling the whole time. He approached without a word as if the whole interaction were choreographed. When the man's lips touched Manuel's, he didn't flinch. His shoulders relaxed. His mind unlocked a memory that'd been padlocked a second before.

The house Manuel had grown up in had a green door with amber glass windows. He had a father (Puerto Rican and Salvadoran) and a mother (Dominican). They were happy to have him living at home while he figured out what to do with his life, but there was an unspoken pressure. Manuel had to make something of himself, a man worthy of the sacrifice his parents had made in coming to this country.

"Sorry," Manuel muttered, pulling away. "I just need a second."

Watching her brand bloom was more exhilarating than Celeste had anticipated. She'd been waiting for the world to call back to her, to say it needed and adored her, and though her belief in herself had never wavered, self-confidence was only part of a career. She put out the single featuring Manu-C, and finally the world began singing her song back to her, elevating praises she knew she'd earned.

Her publicist snagged her a *Rolling Stone* cover story and flew her to New York to be photographed. She posed all around the city, in empty parking lots and busy parks. The photographer shot inside her parents' Queens apartment, asking Celeste to lie on the flower-print couch they'd had for decades. The plastic covering stuck to her skin, but the photographer assured her its reflective sheen added to the shot. At her dining room table, the interviewer asked about her relationship with Manuel.

"Yes, I miss him," Celeste responded. "But I'll see him soon. I love Los Angeles, but it's always nice to get back to one's roots. Plus, we'll be spending a lot of time together. He's promoting the album with me."

Between press junkets and performances, Celeste told Manuel of the raucous schoolyards and concrete stoops where she fell in love with music. All the dreaming she did back in New York was coming to fruition, remaking her world. The week before she met Manuel, she'd been searching for a subletter to take over her lease in Los Angeles, frustrated with the city and her stagnant career. She didn't admit her aching loneliness to him, nor the fact that she'd started counting the number of days she'd spent away from her parents in New York, months she'd never get back.

Celeste couldn't share those ugly feelings with anyone, but weeks of faking softened the two strangers. Their relationship was still artificial, but in the way a wax sculpture is: sturdy, life-size, almost natural, but with the potential to temper even more. Eventually their teams decided that romantic partnership wasn't enough. Celeste and Manu-C had to be musical collaborators too. A modern-day Sonny and Cher. June and Johnny. John and Yoko. There, in the studio, she saw glimmers of the real Manuel. His terrible ear for instrumentation, but solid rhythm. Melodramatic lyrics that he delivered with convincing earnestness.

Celeste agreed to appear in his next music video, and they began rehearsal. The choreography was simple enough, and Celeste liked the repetitiveness of the motions. She swung an arm out toward Manuel, coiled it back, and ran it down her body. In one motion, she squatted, spread her knees apart with her palms, and then bounced back up. On the same beat, she and Manuel stepped toward each other.

Manuel was a better dancer now. He was sure-footed. His body was less robotic. The cameras didn't faze him, and he put on a sultry face when they were rolling. But on their third take, he stumbled and hit the floor knees-first. The director called for a ten-minute break.

Celeste reached for a water bottle from craft services. Beside her, background dancers huddled together in nothing but gold-chain bikinis. When Manuel's team had floated the concept, Celeste had told them the outfits were crass. They'd allowed her to wear something else. They must be freezing, Celeste thought.

"I've been remembering more of my life recently," Manuel

said.

"Glad the amnesia's gone, chikibaby," said Celeste.

"The details were slippery, that's all. Now I remember who I was before that morning I met you."

"You're so full of shit," Celeste said and laughed, even though she'd come to believe him.

"But there's one thing . . ." He hesitated. In the pause, the director called them back in-front of the cameras. "Later," he mumbled.

Celeste stared at him, as if her gaze alone might free his words. The possibility that his admission had to do with her fluttered by. After all these hours together, had he glimpsed her real self, a level of visibility that no one else in California had been able to offer?

Manuel kept his mouth shut, his look contemplative and unfocused, but when the director called action, he slipped back into his stage persona and danced.

Nestled in a velvet booth, in the back of a dim restaurant, Robert smiled and pulled Manuel in for a kiss. Only the waiter would notice them, so Manuel gave himself over.

"It'd be nice to see you before the sun sets," Robert said.

"That's a low blow. How can you be so sexy and so cruel all at once?"

Being with Robert helped Manuel remember a life that he thought was a dream. In that life, Manuel lived on a quiet suburban street occasionally interrupted by dogs barking at old couples on their evening stroll or cars rolling down the road. He still didn't know when or how he had acquired the spoils of his career, but the newfound knowledge of his past grounded him. A fear of insanity had sapped the sugar from his fame, but now it was back. He was finally able to enjoy himself. Expensive cocktails tasted sweet on his tongue. He indulged in the parts of Robert that thrilled him: fleece-soft hair, eyes glossy as bowling balls, thighs strong as tree stumps. Anything Manu-C wanted was just a phone call away.

"I was only half joking," Robert said later that night, back in Manuel's penthouse. They were in the shower together. Steam fogged up the glass door. "No one likes feeling like a secret."

He'd seen Robert mostly at night, either out at the club or in his penthouse. Partially it was optics: he didn't need to give the tabloids proof of the allegations he was fighting. But there was also a whisper in the back of his mind, a voice from his past life insisting that Robert should be kept a secret. He wasn't looking for a fling, or a dirty little secret to hold in his chest, but he also didn't know how much he could bear to sacrifice for him.

"I get that," Manuel said. "But I've told you, we can't be so careless. I wish I could, really."

"I'm not asking for anything crazy," Robert said. "Let's just go on a real date. For my birthday. We can just have lunch. Something simple."

"We could lose . . . all this," Manuel said. He was thinking of Celeste. They'd gotten close, and whatever sparkled between them was also real. It was attraction, yes, but more than that, they shared the sort of trust he knew was precious. If she asked to build on it—a real relationship, love—he would try to. And even if they never made that jump, they were dangerously close already, a bond that'd shatter if broken, scarring them both.

Robert said nothing, so Manuel spoke again to fill the ugly silence.

"I'll think about it. Promise."

Then, Manuel and Celeste kissed, and it felt different than the dozens that'd come before.

The label needed content for Manuel's socials, so they both leaned in. Before closing her eyes, Celeste caught his smile. Her lips stretched out to meet his. When the photographer said he'd gotten the photograph, they insisted on a backup, then a third. When the photo went online a few hours later, Manuel and Celeste were still thinking of how real it'd felt, how quickly they'd gone back to pretending once the camera looked away.

Before Celeste knew about Manuel's lover, she saw him.

Their managers sent them out to dinner together at an overpriced spot in Malibu, and after a few glasses of wine Manuel suggested they go out to a club. They'd gone out together a couple of times already. Those nights had devolved into a blurry, joyful mess. Music shocked her body as intensely as the champagne bubbles, the burn of tequila, the sickly sweet colored shots. Celeste enjoyed Manuel's company, and kissing him was still fun, so she said yes.

Manuel cut the line, slipped a couple bills to the bouncer, and led Celeste to velvety couches on the second floor. He moved fluidly through the crowd, expecting attention and expedited service. When he received it, he didn't blink.

"I'll only be a second," he said, before disappearing into the crowd. She sat for a while, sipping on a cocktail, but after fifteen minutes, anger thinned her patience. Manuel had been the one to suggest the club. He was the one who'd reached under the table, squeezed her thigh, and pleaded. She'd only agreed because it was with him, the person who quieted the loneliness that echoed off every building in the city.

It'd been so long since she'd let her hips shake for herself, not as part of a performance. Quería perrear. For real.

Nestled among other sweaty bodies, she felt almost anonymous. Even with her skyrocketing success, she could remain invisible in this club, filled mostly with people who hadn't heard her music. Reggaeton was making its way into the mainstream, but the genre's true devotees had tanned skin and spoke Spanish like she did. Here, at a club mostly rich and white, she could dance freely.

Her hair whipped around as she swayed her body, sidestepping men who tried grabbing her hips or snaking their way around to grind on her. Sweat formed on her brow, and her arches ached from all the movement. A couple of drinks regenerated her, and after a brief break at the still-empty table, she headed onto the dance floor again.

Past the shadowy outlines of strangers' heads, far across the room from her, she spotted Manuel. His head was nuzzled into a man taller than him. Celeste couldn't tell if he was shouting in his ear or kissing his cheek. Flashing club lights illuminated them in hues of red and white for a few seconds at a time. Manuel never looked washed out, even in the brightest flashes. Robert paled under the strobing lights. They drifted away from each other, though only a few inches, before pulling their chests close together again. Their bodies didn't lie.

Celeste considered pushing through the crowd to reach them, to watch them more closely. But she suddenly felt tired, her eyes heavy. A dull ache settled into her lower back, and her cheeks burned like two briquets. The heat was surprising, but undeniable. Celeste was jealous. She left the humid mass of bodies and throbbing bass.

Outside, the breeze cooled her skin. A good friend wouldn't abandon me, she thought, but quickly reminded herself that Manuel wasn't a real friend. They had a business deal, one that was working well and had an expiration date. A music video and two features, and they'd be done. Celeste pushed down the feeling of betrayal. She wanted to keep the peace, and the profit, so even though her cheeks were still on fire, she went back inside.

Manuel was alone, sitting on the couch. He offered her a drink, which she took without a word. When he asked her to dance, she said yes.

At the night's end, Manuel sidled up to Celeste in the backseat of yet another car and placed his head on her shoulder. His eyes were droopy and bloodshot. It was nearly three A.M., and a small layer of dew had formed on the windshield.

"I have to admit something," Manuel said. "There's a reason my past is clearer now. At the show, I met a man. When he called to me, I couldn't remember his name. But his face looked so familiar. And I realized that he was from before I woke up changed. I stared at him, and realized that in my hazy dreamworld, we'd hooked up. I invited him to my dressing room, we had sex. It felt familiar."

"The rumors are true. You're gay."

"Bisexual," Manuel said. "The life he's helping me unlock, it came before I was this star. Before I had all this money and all these fans. It's like I lived it once, long ago. When he asked me to come tonight, I had to."

And then, as if he hadn't said anything strange or out of line, Manuel grinned. "We're amazing together, you and me. The shoot was so much fun."

Celeste shifted her shoulder slightly, but it felt pinned in place by his weight. Her body was heavy, tired from a night of drinking. A headache had begun to set in.

"Please don't tell anyone about Robert," Manuel pleaded. "Not yet."

To protect herself, Celeste had chosen solitude, but when Manuel appeared, looking as lost as she often felt in her adopted city, a crush formed anyway. She could only admit it now, in this car full of drunken honesty, how much she loved that electricity surged between them. He was right: they were amazing together.

"Okay," she muttered. If she could hide her hurt away, she could keep his secret for a few more weeks. She'd try, for her career, and for him.

The driver sped down empty streets until he pulled up in front of Celeste's apartment building. Manuel was sleeping. Celeste gently cradled his head onto the leather so she could slip out.

As his secret-keeper, Celeste heard all the juicy details gossip blogs would have killed or overpaid for. The affair came up again while Manuel was rerecording a couple of verses from a new song. His team thought the lyrics were too sensitive. "I don't care if it's supposed to be a song about Celeste," his manager said. "It's wimpy shit. Where's the sex? Where's the fire?"

"Let's take five," the audio engineer said. Manuel pulled away from the microphone and into the control room. Celeste was mindlessly scrolling on her phone.

"I need advice," Manuel said. For most people she put on an undecipherable mask, but with him her eyebrows scrunched together as she processed every word. She was an exceptional listener—which was likely what made her such an excellent musician. A good ear in the world made for a good ear in the studio.

"Robert wants to go out. In public," Manuel said.

"Want my honest opinion?" Celeste said. "You can't be invisible. You could try a restaurant a bit farther out from the city. But even then I don't think it'd guarantee you wouldn't be seen."

"He's insistent. He wants to go out together. A normal date, he said."

"Weigh the risks," Celeste said.

"Chikibaby," he said. "Of course."

His reassurance, though, must not have been enough. She

texted an hour later.

I was being serious. I don't think you should go to lunch with him.

Two minutes later, she sent another message.

But if you do . . . be careful, okay?

The text confused him. They both knew the stakes. Their bulging bank accounts proved that fans loved them together. So did he. The hours he spent with Celeste were as precious as his drunken nights out or his dates with Robert. With her, he could be his best self. Beloved, powerful, free. He wrote back.

I care about my career. I'm not going to risk it all. You trust me, yeah?

"You never texted me back," Manuel said. Their managers had called them into the label's offices that morning even though they had no standing plans to see each other.

Though she didn't owe him any grace, Celeste found her lips folding into an apology. "I'm sorry."

If Manuel had ever been a normal person, those days had passed. It was unclear how seriously he understood his responsibility to those around him, people whose lives were tethered on his choices. Celeste had thought that she factored into his equation, but after so many weeks of lying, she couldn't be sure.

"So, here's the problem," Manuel's manager said. "The internet hates your video. They're calling it tired, misogynist trash."

The music video had dropped at midnight, but it'd already garnered thousands of angry comments and dislikes on YouTube.

The backlash focused on the scantily clad women chained in a warehouse, who appeared in hurried clips throughout the video.

"We can say it's a play on the knight-saves-the-princess trope, but I don't think the public will buy that," Manuel's manager said.

"I don't understand why everyone is on my ass about this," Manuel said. "There are women in chains everywhere. No one's complaining about Princess Leia in *Return of the Jedi*."

"I told you to rethink the concept," Celeste said. "You green-lit it anyway."

She felt all the eyes in the room on her. The three men stared at her like she was their salvation.

"Can you post about it on your Instagram?" Manuel asked. "If you tell the world I'm sorry—which I am—it'll help a ton. And then I can go back to my regular life and worry about finishing the next album and our song."

Manuel hadn't hesitated. He knew how she'd feel about the request, but he was also aware of what his career endowed him with. Back when she'd agreed to their arrangement, she sensed a certain humility in him. If not meekness, then fear of how much power he wielded, a sliver of which Celeste wanted for herself. Either she'd misread him—a rarity, but a possibility—or he'd changed course. They were like two drivers on the highway who glimpsed each other through their windows, moving in the same direction on a finite stretch of road, safe in their own contained worlds but changed by the way light fell on the stranger's face, their fates interconnected briefly until one driver turned onto the off-ramp.

Someone had left a copy of Celeste's *Rolling Stone* issue in the conference room. The picture they'd chosen for the cover captured her sitting on the hood of a taxicab, holding a bat. Broken glass covered the floor, and her lyrics were graffitied on the exterior in pink spray paint. The photograph encapsulated the image she'd spent so long curating.

"This is the last favor," Celeste finally said. Their breakup was two weeks away. She could fake it a bit longer.

Nothing made Manuel feel more famous than driving ninety down the highway, fighting a hangover, a vibrant California landscape blurring in the window. With one hand on the wheel, and the other on Robert's thigh, he was untouchable.

Their destination was a place neither remembered visiting. Manuel found a receipt in his wallet with an address at the bottom. It was forty-five minutes from downtown, in a suburb that bordered Orange County. From pictures online, it wasn't anything fancy, just a couple of tables set up in an outdoor patio. Julie's Café. The anonymity it'd offer them was more precious than any of Manuel's diamond bracelets.

"Thank you," Robert said as they waited for their food. "This is perfect."

"Glad you're happy," Manuel said. "You haven't been here before, have you?"

"Never. I have an aunt who lives a couple of towns over, but I've never stopped here."

"It feels familiar," Manuel said. The hazy fog had lifted weeks ago, and in the bustle of his life, he'd forgotten how deeply he'd questioned his own life. But now, in this place—so normal, so domestic, so unlike the life he'd built for himself—a shadow of doubt snuck back. "Must be the décor."

"I read an article about Celeste yesterday," Robert said. "About how her godmother died and left her a CD collection that helped her fall in love with music."

"Mm," Manuel mumbled through a bite of sandwich. He'd never heard that story. Was it real or a publicist's heart-wrenching invention?

"She also mentioned you. Your relationship. How long do you have to keep the act up?"

"Just until we're both where we want to be."

"That's vague."

"It's supposed to be over in a couple weeks, but you know how quickly things shift," Manuel said.

"And she's okay with that?"

Manuel had seen less of Celeste recently, but he viewed it as a temporary blip. They didn't have any active projects, outside of the occasional press appearance.

"If she had an issue, she'd say it. I'm not forcing her into anything."

"It's hard to feel fully with you when the tabloids say you're dating someone else."

"We're having fun, right? No need to sink a good thing," Manuel said. He really did like Robert, but he'd worked hard for his career. He couldn't up give his lifestyle, not for Robert, or Celeste, or anyone else.

"You're right," Robert said after a slow sip of coffee. "Nothing wrong with taking it one day at a time."

Back in the glass-walled conference room, Celeste thought they were meeting to finalize the breakup. It was eight months since they'd met and their fans were invested, so the split had to be calculated but believable.

Manuel avoided eye contact. Celeste added it to his list of transgressions. Manu-C's bad-boy bravado had turned into recklessness. A whirlwind of blind drinking and thousand-dollar tabs followed him in and out of strip clubs and bars. He went out every night. He liked the expensive cars, and expensive drinks, and women who dressed in expensive clothing and circled around him. Celeste read about it online, and when confronted, Manuel didn't deny the claims.

When she still couldn't catch his gaze, Celeste knew something was up. It was an ambush. Manuel had been photographed with Robert the other day, and their hands had been orbiting each other's, which was more than enough to reignite the rumors around Manuel's sexuality. The meeting was to convince Celeste that continuing the farce was still mutually beneficially.

"No," Celeste said when the managers finished talking in circles and vague generalities and finally asked her to fake the relationship a bit longer. "I know Manuel's album is coming out soon, but after that, you'll find another excuse to keep us together."

The line between Manuel and Manu-C had blurred completely. If the other man was still inside him, Manu-C had burrowed him away. He strutted through the world as a megastar now, protecting the life he'd built, forgetting that its scaffolding had once felt like a dream. His and Celeste's slippery bond—fierce friends, almost lovers—had wilted under his wandering eye. She was asking him to do what was right.

"No, I'm out," she said.

Manuel stayed quiet. Celeste's eyes burned into him, but he looked away, just as he had the first time they'd met. The nervous energy he'd given off then was fresh in her mind: pronounced lines on his forehead, his shoulders held up high and tight. He was calm now. Unreadable. He had to know he held the power to offer Celeste peace of mind, even if it'd require sacrifice on his part. Finally, he turned to her.

"I want to keep it going," he said. "Celeste, will you do this—for me?"

On their first date, among the excessive and startlingly clean buildings at the Grove, she'd been surprised how ordinary he looked, as if he were a neighbor from her little spot in Queens, the kind of person who'd understand when she confessed how the storefronts' subtle changes made her sad whenever she flew back to New York. Someone who understood that the past can be an anchor or a bludgeon, depending on how one wields its weight. Instead, Manuel's claws grasped at the future. His future, not theirs.

Celeste stared into Manuel's eyes, wordless, praying for some remorse to bubble up and confirm that she had not been wrong about him all those months ago, that he had in fact changed.

Celeste awoke in bed, after a long night of uneasy dreams, with a half-naked man next to her. The scene would have been the unspectacular aftermath of sex, except that Celeste had never slept with Manuel. And yet there he was, breathing quietly in bed next to her. He didn't have a single tattoo on his body.

Half-asleep, she grabbed her phone and read the dozen messages she'd received overnight. She pulled up *Billboard* to confirm that it was true. Celeste was officially the most-streamed female reggaeton artist of all time, and her most popular song had gone multi-platinum.

She stepped out of bed, still wearing the gray sweatpants and camisole she'd worn to sleep. When Manuel walked into the kitchen, rubbing his eyes, she was sipping from a mug of coffee. She looked at him in the soft light of the midmorning sun, now fully clothed. Though she wanted desperately to ask what he was doing in her apartment, she already knew he wouldn't have an explanation. She was sure he'd been a reggaeton star, felt certain that she hadn't dreamt everything they'd been through. And still, that reality was hazy. It was the feeling he'd described on their first date. He stared back knowingly. An inexplicable transformation had transpired and then come undone.

Together, they scrolled through their phones and scoured the internet for any reference to Manu-C and his career. They clicked through tabloids, Reddit sub-threads, YouTube videos, Instagram pages, conspiracy theorists' blogs, and fan-fiction websites. Manu-C was nowhere to be found. He'd existed, and then he hadn't. Celeste remembered details from their illogical and inevitably fraught relationship, but there wasn't a crumb to be found online.

Her fame was common knowledge, but what she'd torn from herself to achieve it would go unseen.

Manuel told her that after their meeting, he'd fallen asleep in the Hollywood penthouse they both knew was no longer his. She offered to drive him to his parents' house. He now knew, without a doubt, that it's where he'd lived, before the dream. He thanked her multiple times for the ride. Gratitude was a strange, but welcome, addition to their dynamic.

As they walked toward Celeste's Mercedes, a photographer pointed his camera at them from across the street. They were in conversation—avoiding talk of what had happened and instead debating the quality of the latest Bad Bunny album—so they didn't notice the shuttering of the lens. The next day there'd be headlines like "Reggaeton Superstar Celeste Spotted Leaving Hollywood Apartment with Unidentified Hottie." Eventually, the news cycle would sniff out Manuel's name and he'd become *Celeste's lover, 23-year-old Manuel Cisneros*, and he'd get visits in the suburbs, even though he and Celeste communicated almost exclusively online and through text messages. The obsession with cracking who he was and whether he was or wasn't dating the darling of the reggaeton world would bring him clout. He'd gain a social media following, and he'd be offered ludicrous lumps of money to promote products. He'd orbit on the periphery of fame, enjoying its benefits, and Celeste would watch and wonder if this meant they were fated to a lifetime of mini-catastrophes.

But that morning, the photographer hid well. Manuel was

chivalrous, opening the door for Celeste, sparking the rumors in the first place, though his action had little intention behind it. She got behind the wheel, turned the ignition, and pulled out toward the main boulevard. Manuel turned on the radio. One of Celeste's songs was playing. They laughed, together. Neither of them turned it off. The song would end, the next would play, the bass breaking any tension left over, the silence between them transformed.

AN ALTERNATE HISTORY OF EL SALVADOR OR PERHAPS THE WORLD

SELENA QUINTANILLA ENDED UP BEING A complete burnout, even though she'd first hit the scene with a promising single and a bucketload of potential. She released "Contigo Quiero Estar," and listeners were charmed by the dynamic: a female lead singer fronting a band composed of her siblings. "The Mexican Jackson 5," someone wrote in a seldom-read music magazine. She released an album and began to build a fan base, but eventually the hype died out and she was all but forgotten.

A couple of years later she made local headlines again, but this time it had nothing to do with her music. A mega-fan of hers, a woman by the name of Yolanda Saldivar, had gotten into a disagreement with Selena over business dealings. In a fit of rage or obsessive fanhood, Saldivar brandished a .38-caliber Taurus Model 85 at the pop star and threatened to shoot. Luckily, a passerby noticed the altercation and tackled Saldivar, knocking the gun out of her hand and into a nearby sewer drain. Police arrived, Saldivar was arrested, and Selena Quintanilla left unscathed, but plenty spooked. She released no more albums after the incident.

In 1996, a fifteen-year-old Salvadoran American teen stumbled across an old Selena CD in her neighborhood Goodwill. It cost her fifty cents, and it changed her life. She fell in love with that album, and throughout high school she taught herself to read and write music. She moved to New York for college to pursue music and managed to fill a niche in the music industry that was still empty. Her stage name was her first name—Celine— and soon she was given a variety of titles: cumbia queen, Latina

pop princess, an immigrant parent's dream. She gained a repu-
tation as a charming, wholesome young woman. Many of her
fans saw her as a representation of themselves: the children of
immigrants, second-generation Latinos who found themselves
caught between their country and their parents' homelands.

A few months before the release of her third album, Celine
was riding in the backseat of a Mercedes-Benz driven by a member of her publicity team. They rode through West Hollywood,
down Santa Monica Boulevard, late at night. The past few hours
had been spent in the recording studio, and now she was on her
way to meet a friend at a Westwood bar. The driver in the car
that hit hers had been drinking, and he was killed on impact.
Celine's chauffer suffered three fractured ribs but lived. Celine
didn't. The autopsy surmised that she'd been killed on impact
too.

For months, fans placed flowers, balloons, candles, teddy
bears, and crosses on the curbside where Celine had died. Minuscule shrines popped up like wildflowers, and the mourning
cemented Celine as one of the most important Latina artists
of all time. Her record sales skyrocketed, and her music label
quickly released a new greatest hits album that included the
best-selling singles from her first two albums, alongside tracks
from the unreleased third record. Two decades after her death,
a popular fast-fashion retail chain released a series of graphic
T-shirts and sweaters with her image on them.

As part of her debut album, Celine had re-recorded Selena's
"Como la Flor." The cover was one of the standout hits from the
album, and concertgoers would shout the lyrics along as Celine
performed. Posthumously, it was her best-selling single. Selena
had heard the cover for the first time on the radio, just a few
months after Celine had released it. It'd sent a pang of jealousy
through her, but she eventually came to follow the young Salvadoran singer's career in a show of genuine support. The song's

success didn't significantly increase the amount of Selena's royalty checks, but she didn't care. She simply hadn't been destined to be the nation's Latina sweetheart. Selena Quintanilla was okay with that.

MY ABUELA,
THE PUPPET

HAVE BEEN A FAN OF METAPHOR since I learned to read, first in English and then eventually in rusty, copper Spanish. This is not a metaphor. My grandma has become a puppet.

Abuela's body started to change, slowly, ten years ago. Though she was human then, her physique lent itself to a description of a marionette. She had clunky white orthopedic shoes that looked oversize and cartoonish when she took her small, concerted steps. Abuela's back was permanently hunched over, as if she were suspended by invisible strings at the shoulders. She lost a lot of weight, and the lack of fat in her face combined with her wrinkled skin made her head look huge. But Abuela was still herself then, flesh and bones and dust.

When she became a puppet, no one knew what to do about it. Papi wouldn't admit it, but there were signs that her metamorphosis was coming. It wasn't just those dreadful orthopedic shoes.

For a long time, Abuela lived in an apartment by herself. Her relationship with my abuelo had been another one of the precious things lost to migration, and she never bothered dating again. She had her children, who joined her in Los Yunai Estais after she'd been cleaning houses, theaters, and embassies for nearly a decade, for nearly minimum wage. But, of course, Papi and his siblings had grown up and left Abuela in that mustysmelling apartment building. She initially resisted the arrangement but preferred it to a nursing home. Abuela had always valued her independence.

We visited her one afternoon and couldn't avoid the putrid

smell that'd snuck into her home. The whole building smelled of old person. Less kindly: The carpet and walls reeked of dying. But that morning, the odor in Abuelita's apartment stank of something already dead. In the fridge there were rotten casseroles and the unquestionable stink of not-so-fresh queso fresco. Papi managed to save five slices from the loaf of bread, but everything else went into the trash.

Abuela claimed she hadn't smelled the food going bad. Her nose hardly worked anymore, she told us in an attempt to gain our pity. We went with her to the supermarket and bought a cartful of groceries. Two weeks later, they still sat in the fridge, largely untouched and mostly spoiled. I'm just not hungry, she told us when confronted. Over the next couple of months, we repeated the routine, giving her the benefit of the doubt, until her arms began to look like a well-loved rag doll's.

Eventually Mami convinced Papi to let Abuela move into our home in the suburbs. Abuela said they were being ridiculous, that she was fine in her apartment, that she was happy. But Mami was worried she'd fall one day and that no one would be there to help her. The weight loss worried her. Abuela had a large gut throughout my childhood, the kind that makes you wonder what would happen if you tipped her over and tried rolling her down the street. But by the time she moved into my old bedroom, her gut was gone. If you tipped her over, she'd plop onto the sidewalk like a plank of wood.

There's a purse Abuela loves. It's a knockoff Louis Vuitton that she picked up in MacArthur Park a year or so before the rotting fridge fiasco. When she became a puppet, a version of the bag stayed stitched to her side, though it was made of felt and had less detail than the original. The print has lost all its definition. The letter and shapes are indistinguishable from one another, forming no more than a muddled slate of gold and brown fabric. But the purse sticks to her side, even as she lies tossed over a chair.

Before she was a puppet, Abuela swung that purse around and hit Papi straight across the cheek, leaving him with neck pains he'd complain about for weeks. She was accusing him of stealing money from her. Papi assured her that, no, he hadn't touched her wallet, but she continued. She remembered putting a stack of twenty-dollar bills in the small pocket of her purse, and now she couldn't find it. Papi had stolen them, she yelled, the ungrateful hijuesupadre. She pulled back her flabby arm and took aim, slamming the purse hard against his face.

In his moment of shock, Abuela made a run for it. She pushed past me, with a strength that her limp marionette arms no longer possess. The woman who sang me lullabies about baby chicks and coyotes lay her hands on me without any tenderness. She opened the front door and ran out into the rain-soaked neighborhood with her Louis Vuitton fake.

I stayed in the doorway to her bedroom, immobile. Abuela had fallen into moments of rage before, but the normal kind anyone is susceptible to. She barked at waiters when they forgot my order. At weddings, or funerals, she joked when it was clear I or my cousins needed a pick-me-up. Her love was clear, quietly expressed in both words and actions. She cared for me, had never hurt me before. When she shoved me, I froze under the chill of a betrayal I'd fight to forget, even after it became clear that her body was betraying her. Rationalizing the hurt didn't make it disappear. I wanted to cry.

Mami and Papi got into the minivan and went out searching for her. They spotted her through a sprinkled windshield, waiting at the wrong bus stop. Her plan, my parents told me after I'd wiped the bags under my eyes dry, was to ride the bus back to her apartment. She had forgotten the bus route to get there, though she'd ridden it for nearly a decade. It'd slipped her mind that she no longer had a lease on that musty pink apartment.

The home we moved Abuela into after the seventy-five-year-old runaway situation didn't smell of dying. It was sterile, and the hallway of doors where hers stood was fenced off from the rest of the living facility. A brass gate separated those who could remember and those who couldn't. Abuela lived in the section for people whose memories were turning into small wisps, ready to float away from their temples into the clouds. A nurse would press a four-number code into a small keypad, and the door would let us through.

Each tenant had their own room, but they all took their meals in a large open-floor dining area. The nurses would go knock on Abuela's door when it was dinnertime if she hadn't arrived to eat. Her mind was a lost cause, but there was no reason her body had to be as well.

Every visit gave us clues that we ignored. Silence was our heritage. What Abuela taught Papi, he passed on to me. Even a change as shocking as Abuela's couldn't break the chain. One day Papi asked Abuela how she used to make Christmas tamales. Being the man's man that he is, he'd never stepped in the kitchen to actually make the dish. But he knew the steps well enough to know that his mother had forgotten them completely.

A professor had assigned an oral history project, so I'd decided to interview Abuela about the war and the way it had shaped her migration. She began telling me the story, and the most graphic of details were sharp and clear. She recounted how an army soldier took a machete to a pregnant woman's stomach because they feared that her baby was a communist. She told me that the guerrilleros befriended her favorite cow and three days later murdered it for the meat.

When I prompted her to tell me her immigration story, she had to correct herself. Papi, who was sitting just a few feet away, eventually led her along, reminding her that she'd gone to Puerto Rico before moving to Miami. He explained that he'd stayed in El Salvador for the first two years she'd been in San Juan, an abandoned child reemerging in his tenor.

Soon she didn't know our names. She called us all mijo or mija. Eventually she opted to simply use "linda," regardless of the gender of the person she was speaking to. Slowly, we became nearly strangers to her. My grandmother treated us the way she'd treat the mailman or a friend's relative she was meeting for the first time. There was a sense of trust, but nothing more.

Though Abuela was human on all those trips, I pretended she wasn't. Like the other people in this caged home for the forgetful, she'd lost her stories. I'd smile a hollow smile at the other residents, tell Abuela that I loved her even though I knew she didn't recognize me, and then slink away to a corner of the room. Abuela was alive on a technicality, hovering on the razor-thin edge of life, but I, stupidly, feigned indifference, as if distance would protect me.

A nurse noticed the change first. Whenever he helped Abuela to the bathroom, she left wool tufts on the bedsheets. The nurse figured they were from an old sweater until the tufts began appearing elsewhere: the shower curtain, the courtyard, her wheelchair, the floor of the dining hall. Every time he pulled her up by the forearms, she felt lighter. Soon he told us they could no longer care for her at the facility. Abuela had to come home again.

By then I had moved out to start my Ph.D., and despite knowing they could have used an extra hand around the house, I didn't offer. School was busy, sure, but I stayed away out of cowardice. I didn't want to risk repeating the pain of that rainy afternoon, even if Abuela was weaker. Less herself.

I watched my parents care for Abuela as she slowly changed. When she completely lost the ability to walk, Papi hoisted her in his arms and carried her to the toilet, with a huff and a series of small steps. She got lighter and lighter, until he could pick her up without any effort. Mami took over the duty then, and when the situation was dire, I would step in. Abuela puckered in my arms like a pile of sheets.

Her sentences became less lucid, until she began repeating the same words over and over. Eventually she lost the ability to speak entirely, swapping coherent phrases for a string of muffled noises. Her jaw fell unhinged, then rose again, and then down once more, the same mumble escaping every time. Now I'm realizing that maybe Abuela was speaking the clandestine language puppets speak when a ventriloquist isn't pulling at their lips.

Then one morning the noises stopped completely. Her mouth shut and never opened again. She was a puppet.

Papi and Mami refused to bury her. She's not dead, they'd insist, even though we all saw where nylon strings met her joints. Mami grabbed my hand and pressed it against Abuela, commenting on her warmth. My fingertips caressed the nest of fibers that made up her skin, which was no warmer than the couch. Her flesh no longer felt like old leather. It was softer, nicer even, but less human, even if my parents wouldn't admit it. I pulled my fingers away quickly.

Mami and Papi parented me for eighteen years, and soon after, they had to swaddle and nurse Abuela like a newborn. She'd spent years leaving us, transforming into this new form, but still wanted more. If she'd died, we could have mourned her together, but figuring out what to do with her puppet put us at an impasse. It was unfair. I couldn't bring myself to extend the mourning period any longer, especially with the possibility that my parents might inherit whatever changed Abuela. I said a private goodbye to the grandmother I'd known and tried to accept that she'd never return.

Abuela the Puppet hung in my parents' home for years. They couldn't move on, even if they no longer changed dirty diapers or lived in fear of a broken bone. Eventually my parents and I stopped arguing. Even though she'd gone completely still, Abuela would stay.

Abuela watched over us from a hook in our living room, hovering as we watched television, ate dinner, and got into quiet arguments, not wanting to be disrespectful. If she moved, it was because a breeze was blowing through an open window. She was the only one who saw when I snuck a man into the house when I was staying over during Christmas break.

Most days she just hung there, but one weekend, when I was visiting from graduate school, she began to sing. Her voice was stronger and clearer than it had been for years before her transformation.

"*Ay, ay, ay, ay, canta, y no llores. Porque cantando se alegran, cielito lindo los corazones.*"

It was my favorite song as a child, so I knew she was singing it just for me. My parents stared at me with a concerned look when I told them. When I tugged at Abuela's strings and moved her mouth up and down with my hands, trying to prove to my parents what I'd heard, she didn't budge. My grandmother remained limp and unmoving. My father placed a wrinkled hand on my shoulder and told me that it might be a sign that I had that memory-denigrating termite Abuela suffered from for so long. It usually skipped a generation.

Mami and Papi died sixteen months apart, leaving me to deal

with my grandmother. It'd been nearly a decade since Abuela had gone silent. Illnesses took my parents too, but in a twisted way I was grateful for the quickness of their ailments. One died. Before I could fully come to terms with the loss, another left me. I was alone, but there was no drawn-out affair. The shock was preferable to the painful anticipation of a goodbye. The pain would be there regardless, but at least I wouldn't hate myself for wishing it'd come sooner.

Abuela hung in my childhood home as I packed Mami and Papi's possessions into boxes to be thrown away or donated. Abuela said nothing as I held every object, deciding whether it was worth keeping for the memories it held. I hated her. I hated her so much for taking so much space for so long, for forgetting my name, for making a fool of me with her lullaby. I hated her for the termites she'd left in my brain, and for all the pain she was going to put my children through. At church services, a newly reintroduced part of my routine, I prayed for death. God, diosito lindo, please don't make me a puppet.

I've finally decided to get rid of Abuela. I was scrolling online when the algorithm sent me an advertisement for a company that indefinitely stores family members in Abuela's condition. They've bought out an old lot of storage units and repurposed them to accommodate rows and rows of human-size puppets. Most of the puppets are immigrants from war-ravaged places, and the facility groups people together by country of origin.

As I walk through the lot, flanked on either side by corrugated metal doors, Abuela is slung over my shoulder. An employee guides me toward the back of the facility. Abuela's not heavy, but I'm still careful. I make sure she's right-side up, and that her plastic eyes face the sky. I want her to see the blue, beautiful expanse of the heavens—not the washed-out gray asphalt underneath my feet. The storage rooms will be dark, pitch-black, and though Abuela hasn't spoken since she sang for my ears only, I want her last view of the world to be beautiful.

The employee points to a storage unit on our right. In thick black brushstrokes, the door is marked CENTRAL AMERICA. She walks over to the side where there's a keypad. A buzzer sounds when she punches in the code, and the door creaks open. Inside, I can see rows and rows of caramel grandmothers displaced from the isthmus. They hang loosely on copper racks, their faces made of wrinkled felt. The air is stale, silent.

Carefully, I hand Abuela to the employee, who takes her and swings her like she's nothing more than a moth-infested coat. With a quick hand, she pushes the puppets into each other to make more room. She hangs Abuela on the rack. Back outside, the employee clicks a button on the keypad, and gears squeak alive. As the door to the storage unit closes, Abuela's jaw twitches. No sound comes out, so I imagine a beautiful melody, whispered just for me.

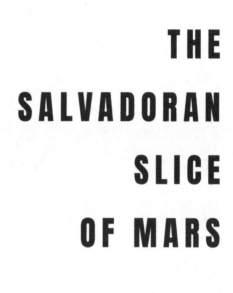

THE
SALVADORAN
SLICE
OF MARS

OUR HERO IS TRAPPED IN A detention center on Mars. Outside, the horizon spreads out in an endless plateau, interrupted only by an occasional rocky hill or the outline of Nuevo Cuscatlán. Near sunset, when the sky turns a fiery orange, the landscape is almost Earth-like, mimicking the desert in Blythe, that migrant-filled town on the California-Arizona border. The United States' latest border town. The town where our hero last saw his parents.

Earlier, he met a friend from work—another undocumented bricklayer—at a seedy bar. Things were looking up, our hero told him. His parents had gotten word that they'd be allowed into Arizona in a few days, which meant that a reunion might be possible. They still had to figure out whether he'd return to Earth, or if it'd be best for them join him on the colony, but either way, they'd be reunited soon.

Our hero was giddy. He drank Pilsners imported from Earth. He never much liked the beers when he'd lived in El Salvador as a teenager, but now they reminded him of the stability of those years. He joked, for the first time in months, and let the buzz rise to his head.

And then, in the sort of split-second encounter that changes a life, an immigration officer overheard our hero singing to himself in English on his way home. The officer scanned his false passport, and when the machine let out an ugly beep, he clamped handcuffs down hard on our hero's wrists. Our hero pleaded, saying he was Salvadoran. He'd lived half his life in the country. He used vos instead of usted and knew how sweet mamones are freshly plucked off the branch. His Americanness was more about circumstance than desire.

None of that mattered to the immigration officer.

In the cell, the only light comes from under the doors, one on each wall. The cinder blocks sport a streaky paint job. It smells of hydrogen peroxide and blood. Even in the shadows, our hero can tell all the other Americans are white. Without saying anything to his cellmates, he lays his skull against the cold concrete. His skin, once sun-kissed and salted with ocean spray, is stark against the eggshell paint.

Before he was a Martian outlaw, our hero lived in Los Angeles, then La Libertad. He was born at USC Verdugo Hills, where his mother was a part-time professor of architecture. She was a bit of a hotshot, famous for designing the stilted neighborhoods all along the California coast, so much so that our hero's father nicknamed her "the Architect." The pet name stuck, even when our hero was old enough to realize that wasn't his mother's legal name.

Our hero's passport had a glinting gold eagle, but on his eighth birthday, the Architect moved their family to El Salvador. She'd signed a contract with the Salvadoran government that'd lift hundreds of homes into the air and away from the encroaching oceans. It was an act of philanthropy meant to offset the millions she'd made elevating rich people's beachside properties in California.

"I'll be at the beach often to scout out the coastline," the Architect told our hero. "You can come play in the sand."

The sea changed over the years, from a translucent turquoise peppered with white taffy sea-foam to a cloudy brown. All the while, our hero watched from the sand, though he desperately wanted to swim in the waves. The sand irritated him, coating him like a layer of shedding skin. Grains of sand fell from his scalp into his eyes, making them water. The boy wanted more.

Our hero resisted for a while. The oceans were acidifying due to an unmitigated release of carbon into the atmosphere. Coastal cities had begun putting out advisories against swimming in the ocean after children began flooding into hospitals with severe skin irritation. The Pacific was becoming more and more destructive, even if the United States and allied governments refused to admit it. (Neither the Republican nor Democratic presidential platforms mentioned anthropogenic climate change that year.)

Eventually, though, the vast expanse was irresistible. Not even the Architect's warnings could stop him.

He sprinted into the ocean, his soles sinking into the soft sand below the waves. Water sprinkled up to hug his thighs, and soon he was waist-deep. He dove in headfirst. The ocean was warm. He stared at the sky until he saw sunspots, then dipped his entire body back into the sea. The water felt good on his thick curls. There was nothing better than this feeling of lightness, as if gravity had stopped working. Our hero told himself he'd forever love the ocean.

When his eyes began to water, he assumed it was the salt. His body was unfamiliar with the sea, so it'd naturally take a bit of time to adjust. He shut his eyes to alleviate the pain. His skin stung too, building to a full-on burn. It became unbearable, so he cried out and flailed his arms.

Doctors treated his irritated skin for over a week. Small boils formed on his skin, and some of them had gotten infected in the time it took to get to the hospital in San Salvador. The boils popped, oozing creamy yellow pus. His arms and legs were splotchy and red, and they burned as a nurse applied ointment and bandages. He cried and cried, his tears leaving streaks on his cheeks that smelled of brine.

After he recovered, our hero refused to go to the beach, not even to sit in the glowing sand. When the ocean accelerated its encroachment on coastlines all over the world, he was inundated with images of waves crashing down on cement and asphalt. More cities on stilts were created, and his family continued to cash in.

These were also the years when the Lower North American Federation (LNAF) coalesced. After Mexican scientists observed waves eating the edges of the Yucatán Peninsula, they lobbied public officials throughout the isthmus until the governments of Mexico, Belize, El Salvador, Guatemala, Costa Rica, Nicaragua, Honduras, and Panama agreed to search for joint solutions to the existential threat at their shores. When the efforts to colonize Mars began, LNAF's Projecto Ares was the front-runner.

As our hero got older, the memory of his swim became fainter. He regained an appreciation for the ocean: the way it mimicked the color of the sky, its incomprehensible size and seeming endlessness, how it ignored humans' attempts to separate themselves from it. It wouldn't be until he'd made it to Mars that he could admit how much it had taken.

Our hero has no idea how long he's been sitting in the freezing Martian cell. The guards slide measly beige scoops of rice through a slot in the door. They remove detainees for interrogation, but most don't return. The LNAF claims deportations back to Earth are humane, even though they condemn people to an increasingly inhabitable planet. There are dozens of stories of outlaws who meet cruel endings at the hands of immigration officers, leaving the colony in body bags.

Our hero squints his eyes, trying to make out the features of the men tied up next to him, when a thud rings out through the room.

"What the hell are you doing?" a redheaded American yells. A man named Bradley is banging his head against the concrete walls, and though others chime in urging him to stop, he doesn't. Our hero understands. Trapped in the dark, with only their thoughts, guilt, and regrets, this is where they're all headed eventually.

Suddenly the blinding ceiling lights burst on. Blood drips down the side of Bradley's face. Pink flesh pokes out. Dime-size stains speckle the wall. Our hero wonders if his own flesh would look as rosy peeking out from under his tanned skin.

A door swings open, and a pair of guards hurl the sort of expletives favored by teenagers who called themselves Chicano on Earth. One grabs Bradley by the front of his bloodstained shirt, and though he slackens his body in resistance, the guards drag him out of the cell and slam the door shut behind them.

In desperation, our hero stands, his arms handcuffed behind his back. He throws his weight against the door. It's a fruitless, doomed action, only slightly less mad than Bradley's self-mutilation, but he does it anyway. The metal is cold against his shoulders, somehow colder than the room that chills the detainees from their skin inward. The handle clatters, but the door doesn't budge.

When Bradley is thrown back into the cell, the detainees murmur at the sight of him. Hastily wrapped bandages hug his face, but blood still soaks through. He slumps to the floor, pupils unfocused.

"Who's stirring shit up in here?" the guard shouts. "We have a way of dealing with shit-stirrers, you know."

He steps toward our hero.

"Was it you?" the guard asks. His tobacco-tinged breath reeks, and his green jumpsuit is spotted with brown stains. Our hero steps back, until his crisscrossed wrists press up against a wall. The guard is shorter, thinner, and dirtier than him, but holds all the power. He pushes our hero, who stumbles.

It's an opening—a small hint of light in the unwavering dark-ness. One by one, the detainees get on their feet. Hands tied, they throw themselves against the guard. Outnumbered, he falls to the floor, desperately reaching for his radio. Our hero kicks it out of his hand. The other men stomp the guard's chest and stomach until he's unconscious.

Powered by adrenaline and the vague hope that they'll re-construct the way out of the building, the nine men jog down the hallway, their shoes squeaking on the white antiseptic floors. Our hero struggles to keep his balance. Cold metallic handcuffs pinch his wrists. Escape is unlikely, but he must try.

Before he boarded a cargo rocket to Mars, and before he was our hero, he was like many seventeen-year-olds. He watched dubbed anime and played first-person shooters with his friend down the street. Typical almost-adult stuff filled his days, until El Desastre shattered the stability he'd come to rely on.

Our hero's family moved back to El Salvador so the Architect could make minor adjustments to her original designs. In the initial plans, she'd spent hours considering the best materials for the foundation, knowing they'd be built directly into bedrock that'd soon be covered by quickly acidifying water. Given the scarcity of materials in the Salvadoran coastal towns—compared to a North American city like New York—she'd suggested ma-terials that'd resist corrosion but would be cheaper to buy. The redesigns were simply meant to reinforce the elevated cities.

But the Architect didn't account for how quickly fossil fuel deregulation took hold. The Paris Agreement fell apart com-pletely. The U.S. government funded an international cam-paign that championed fracking and tar sand pipelines. Global superpowers turned the oceans into toxic stew, while denying that they were affecting it at all.

The Architect's cities came tumbling down. For weeks, headlines haunted her and her family: "El Desastre de La Libertad Kills 102 Salvadorans," "Residents of Stilted Cities Displaced Inland," "American Engineer Recommendations Threatened Structural Integrity of Stilted Cities." When she saw a photograph of a child's shoulder poking out from underneath a pile of rubble, she threw up in the patio garden. Our hero watched as she wiped the vomit off the corner of her mouth, only then understanding the severity of his mother's miscalculation.

"The articles are only getting worse and worse," our hero's father said, reading an op-ed claiming that the Architect's ineptitude was a sign of American arrogance and disrespect for the Salvadoran people.

"I can't let them treat me this way," the Architect said. "I've already paid out the settlements. Dios mío. They can't keep blaming me like this."

Our hero knew they'd leave El Salvador soon.

As his father packed their bags, he went to say one last goodbye to the coast with his mother. The toes of their sneakers dug into walnut-colored dirt. The sand our hero played in as a nine-year-old had been eaten up by the surf, along with the stilted cities' beams and bolts.

"On the day you went to the hospital with all those shiny red boils," the Architect said, "I thought I reached a low point as a mother. I figured nothing could be worse than that."

"The ocean's still beautiful," our hero said. His mother nodded before responding.

"But it doesn't respect anyone or anything. No buildings, no borders. Nothing."

If they'd been able to stay in El Salvador—if disaster hadn't made them exiles—the Architect and her family might have made it up to Mars together. The LNAF and other countries hit hard by environmental catastrophe combatted anthropogenic climate change, but eventually realized that the future was interstellar. It was no coincidence that those governments were the first to break ground on the Red Planet. The scientists and politicians who had the earliest and clearest path to salvation on Mars were from quickly slimming countries like El Salvador, Panama, the Philippines, Japan, and Antigua.

But our hero and his family fled to the United States under the dying embers of sunset, which reaffirmed that they were in fact Americans. Soon they'd be like thousands of other American families: marooned and desperate, trying to survive on an increasingly unlivable planet.

The doors all along the hallway are locked; smooth, impenetrable walls of metal. The holding cell with the unconscious guard waits behind them. The Americans have no way out. After a few minutes of confused mutters and some arguing, Bradley speaks up. Rusty blood taints his bandaged forehead.

"The guard has a key card," he says.

"You're fucking insane," the redheaded detainee says. "You go and get it."

"I've been through enough today, don't you think?" Bradley says.

"The wetback should go. If the guard wakes up, he'll go easier on him," the redhead says.

Bradley locks eyes with our hero, who stares into his crystalline blue irises to avoid the gazes of the other men. The white man's lips are pressed together, though they twitch in the direction of the cell. It's a signal of sorts, a wordless cosign of the redhead's proposal.

Without a word to the group, our hero walks back toward the cell. He doesn't know what he'll do if the guard is awake waiting for him, but his options are slim. For much of his time on Mars, he's shrunk himself, trying to avoid being caught. Now it's time to really be a hero, to do what he can to live another day.

Our hero steps back into the cell, his skin prickling from both fear and the drop in temperature. The key card hangs from a spring snap on the guard's belt. The radio and a baton lay on the floor a couple yards from him. His eyes are closed.

First the handcuffs. Quietly, our hero gets on his knees next to the guard's neck. He can hear the shallow pulsing of his chest. He lowers his butt toward the floor, leans back, and moves his hands up and down the guard's waist, aiming for the key card, though he can't see where it is. After a few seconds of this, he hears a click and feels the metal loosen, freeing his wrists.

The guard stirs. Our hero panics. Unsure of what else to do, he balls his hands into fists and punches. The first swing skims the bottom of the guard's chin, but the second lands square on his cheek. The motion feels unnatural—vulgar, even—but our hero continues.

Dazed, the guard tries scooting away. Our hero lunges, grasping at the clip on the guard's belt. It snaps open, and his fingers fumble to free the key card. The guard tries pulling him down by the bicep. With an awkward slap, our hero pushes the guard's face away, grabs the radio, and runs out of the cell.

To the white Americans in the hall, our hero looks like a guard, like the men they've learned to avoid on Mars. His jutting nose and brown skin signal danger, but in this moment they must set that aside. Our hero is their salvation.

He presses the key card against one of the many doors and ushers the other Americans through it. The guard's footsteps are loud, but when the door closes, only muffled shouts and pounding come through.

The Americans form a routine: open a door, run through the hallway, open another. Repeat. Our hero leads the way. They aren't exactly working their way out of the detention center, but if they outrun the guard and avoid his coworkers, there's hope.

Our hero pulls open a door with no key card sensor, stupidly hopeful it'll lead to the outside world. It's a storage closet, nothing more.

"It's a dea—" our hero is saying when he's knocked down.

The key card slides across the hospital-like floor. The redhead picks it up and opens another door, and the others run through, abandoning our hero. He bangs and bangs, but the door won't reopen.

Guards are looking for him. His cellmates have double-crossed him. Our hero is stuck in between, with no way out of this hallway. All he's left with is the enemy's radio. In a split-second decision, he shuts himself in the storage closet. He presses his back against the concrete and sinks to the floor. Applying pressure with his whole body, he begs the wall to open and swallow him whole.

For three years, our hero, his father, and the Architect enjoyed a brief respite in Los Angeles. It wasn't perfect. The Architect no longer took jobs designing elevated neighborhoods, and the settlements pulled the family down from the echelons of the hyper-wealthy. The oceans were bloated with carbon, and coastal damming systems regularly broke down, washing thousands of homes out to sea. The edges of the United States were dissolving, but the government wasn't too concerned with extraterrestrial solutions. There was a lot of dry land, and most people were distracted by the demagogues in elected office. Our hero thought his family would be okay in the long run.

But by the end of our hero's twentieth year, the waves had eaten the office building where the Architect first blueprinted the stilted homes in La Libertad. The bricks and shattered windowpanes tumbled down into an ocean that wasn't waning, so our hero and his family loaded their hatchback with a fraction of their possessions and drove east. They figured they could rebuild a home in Arizona, or even farther into the country's heart.

They drove for three hours, past increasingly empty landscapes adorned only with stray desert shrubs. As the sun rose directly above their heads, the highway became narrower. Near one of the rare off-ramps, the hatchback shuddered to a stop.

"We've been here before," the Architect said with a small sigh. "Blythe. We stopped for gas and ate at the McDonald's." A sheriff flashed his lights and instructed them to exit the highway. Our hero saw then how the town had transformed.

Before, Blythe was nothing more than a small, dusty town in the middle of the desert. It was a stop for road-trippers on their way to Phoenix or the Grand Canyon, a convenient place to buy a burger or refill a tank. Now it was a bustling refugee camp. Cars were packed into dirt lots off a crumbling road. Men sat on the hoods of their sedans and in truck beds. Children chased each other in circles, snaking around the RVs and tents that popped up like succulents in the ashy dirt.

The sheriff explained that the only people allowed across the Colorado River were those who'd petitioned for entry in advance. In response to classified reports that California would be submerged within the year, the governors of Arizona, Nevada, and Utah shut their borders, sparking a lawsuit over a constitutional violation of the Fourteenth Amendment.

"You're welcome to apply for special entry," the sheriff said. "Or you can wait to see if the court case works itself out. Best bet would be to do both."

Blythe grew around them. Temperatures skyrocketed during the day and sank below freezing at night. Shantytowns of cinder blocks and corrugated metal formed, and the pile of applications grew taller and taller as thousands of Californians flocked to the border to escape their drowned hometowns. Our hero and his family slept in the hatchback, on uncomfortable car seats, waiting for good news. The coastline crept toward them, moving meters every single day.

In the two months our hero waited, the global crisis escalated. Dry land became a luxury, and most nations closed their major airports. Countries with colonies on Mars funneled their resources into permanently relocating their citizens, sending rocket ship after rocket ship of families spaceward. The Americans hadn't been able to wheedle themselves onto the planet. As the main culprits behind the crisis, and centuries of other, smaller disasters, all Americans were banned.

So our hero waited, knowing that Arizona was the only real option for his family. He befriended a teenager about his age, and though there was little to do in Blythe, they kept each other entertained by drawing pictures in the dirt, until one day the friend said he was leaving.

"To Mexico," he explained. "My parents and I are U.S. residents, but we still have our Mexican passports. They don't think we'll ever get into Arizona, so we're driving to Mexicali tomorrow. And from there, we'll make it up to Mars."

Soon after, the Architect would whisper to our hero, holding back the tremor that threatened to overtake her voice. "The only option is up."

Money was tight, so our hero would have to go alone. His parents would wait in Blythe and figure out a way of reuniting once they got to Arizona.

"We'll be together again soon," the Architect promised. "Either here or up there."

The plastic edge of a janitor's mop bucket digs into our hero's shoulder. Even though he's done nothing for days, in the grimy storage closet a deep exhaustion sets in, similar to the ache from a full day of laying bricks. Never has he had to work so hard for so little. His shirt is soaked in sweat, the cheap cotton gripping the hairs on his chest. The closet is cluttered with cleaning agents and spray bottles, but there's nowhere to hide.

He closes his eyes for a second, but when muffled footsteps and faint voices come from somewhere outside the storage closet, he tries to focus. A pressure builds in our hero's temples. Boots thunder in the hallway. Our hero is acutely aware of how tense his body is. Though he'd been fairly skinny all his life, his biceps widened because of all the construction work. Layers of sinewy muscle tighten.

Then the radio shrieks, betraying our hero. The door swings open.

Our hero grabs the guard's olive coveralls and tries swinging him against the wall. The guard grips his tattered shirt, stretching the cheap fabric in his hands. Soon the two men are locked with their heads against each other. Their cheeks, flushed and rosy, crash as they struggle.

Our hero has never found a thrill in physical violence, not even horseplay, so when he grabs the mop bucket it isn't out of fury or a desire to maim. He simply wants to be free, and it's pure desperation that bashes the wheels against the guard's temple. He falls unconscious.

When the guard doesn't move, our hero lowers his ear to the guard's chest. It's shallow, but he's breathing. Our hero could have killed the guard. This is the kind of man he's become. He dry-heaves at the thought.

If he's going to get out, our hero must use the advantage his cellmates don't have. He unzips the guard's jumpsuit, revealing the bruises that bloom all over his body. He dry-heaves again, but eventually slips into the uniform. The green fabric looks wrong against his brown flesh, but he knows this is the only way out. Disguised, our hero might somehow make it out of the labyrinth.

The false passport felt flimsy in our hero's fingers. He kept his lips pursed tight and passed it to the customs officer at the Guatemala–El Salvador border.

"What's your business in the country?" the official asked.

"Space travel." Our hero hoped the official wouldn't ask more questions.

"On your way to Mars?" The man sighed. "I've seen so many young men come back home, only to leave again."

The Martian colony was the crowning achievement of Projecto Ares. The LNAF terraformed more and more of the planet every day, aided by the hundreds of people arriving monthly. The Nicaraguans worked with the Vietnamese to build aerogel bubbles that'd protect the cities from the endless sandstorms. The Guineans helped the Salvadorans install booths for interplanetary communication. The Mexicans organized law enforcement efforts.

Coalitions made the planet habitable, and then alluring. Everyone wanted to be on Mars, but since resources were limited—mining asteroids and importing materials from Earth wasn't easy—the LNAF and its allies had to set some rules. One of them had to do with visa requirements. Only those who could produce a birth certificate proving they were born in an allied country were eligible for passage to Mars.

Our hero bummed around El Salvador on mostly empty buses, searching for a solution to his dilemma. He stayed wherever he could find the cheapest lodging, his funds thinning. In one small town—adorned with nothing more than a church an abandoned plaza—he borrowed a phone to call his parents. Nothing much had changed for them. They were still waiting to hear if they'd be allowed passage into Arizona.

Hope came soon after. A man in a fedora approached our hero as he shoveled down the first full meal he'd eaten in days.

"They tell me you're on your way to Mars," he said. The man was in his forties, and he had a patchy beard and a couple of missing teeth. The others were yellowed and stained by the cigarettes in his breast pocket. "I can help you with that."

The smuggler told him it'd be $9,000, but with no other options, our hero asked his parents if they could wire him the cash, knowing they needed the money as much as he did.

"Whatever it takes," the Architect said. "Just try to call us when you get there. Please."

And so our hero boarded a cargo rocket carrying construction supplies and exported beer. For eight months, he played out all the possible scenarios. He'd live alone on Mars for only a few months, until his parents could join him. Or his mother would find the funds to build a new home for them—indestructible, far above the ocean—and he'd zip back down to Earth. He didn't know then that he'd be trapped in the detention center, unsure if he'd ever escape, if he'd ever see his parents again.

In the minutes before touchdown, our hero looked through the tiny porthole. He was so minuscule in the infinitely expanding universe, and yet there he was: a young man who'd made it off Earth and ventured far enough to see the swirling sandstorms on Mars' face. Infinite possible outcomes, and he'd arrived at the brink of a rebirth, another shot at a dignified life.

Our hero sneaks past real guards who assume he's a new hire. Eventually he finds a door with a window to the outside world. The dusky red landscape has never looked so beautiful. A single vertical barrier, only a few inches thick, stands between him and freedom.

The door is locked. Our hero wants to scream but doesn't.

The door slides open. An immigration officer walks in, dragging a man in by the shoulder. Our hero recognizes the man in cuffs. Their lives overlapped briefly on a construction site. He can't remember his name, but knows the man is in his thirties, Nicaraguan, and from Oakland. Our hero braces himself, waiting for the man to scream and ruin his escape.

But the Nicaraguan's lips purse shut, and his chest tightens, as if he's holding his breath with all his strength. He doesn't resist as he's led down the hallway. Our hero slips out of the front door before it locks, and his boots finally make direct contact with Martian dust.

The opportunity to be courageous was there, then it was gone. Our hero could have tackled the guard and tried bringing the Nicaraguan with him to freedom, but he hadn't. He let the Nicaraguan become who he himself had been: a man freezing in the cell, desperate for escape, unsure if he'd ever see the Martian sunset again.

It was cowardly, but not unexpected, because truthfully, our hero is not a hero at all. He's an outlaw whose only desire is to survive one day longer out in the open, so he acts selfishly. A boy longing for his parents reacts like a child: on impulse, without tact. He's just a man susceptible to the whims of his governments, the one he was born into and the one he adopted. He wears many names—criminal, rule-breaker, laborer, foreigner, ingrate, man, boy, son, refugee—because, really, who can be a hero in the unrelenting tide of injustice?

Red dust speckles his boots as he walks away from the facility. He mounts a motorbike, and the key card in his pocket sparks the engine. In the distance, the skyline of the LNAF colony shimmers. When he arrives, he'll call his parents and make plans. There'll be no time to hesitate, since immigration authorities will be searching for him. Deimos is a speck in the sky.

Phobos is a glowing orb. The desert spans endless in front of him. High above, the aerogel capsule gleams like the surface of a soapy bubble. Among the buildings of Nuevo Cuscatlán, he's built a life. With a rev of the engine, he drives toward it.

AN ALTERNATE HISTORY OF EL SALVADOR OR PERHAPS THE WORLD

AN UNTRACEABLE DISEASE CONFOUNDS SCIENTISTS AND physicians all over the United States. For unknown reasons, the illness discriminates based on national origins. In hospitals from Los Angeles to New York City, Central American immigrants sport hospital gowns as they vomit into bedside pans. Only people who come from the isthmus are affected by the mysterious stomach bug. The Mexicans are fine. The Ecuadorians are fine. The Columbians are fine. The Latin American diaspora is dealing with civil conflict, refugee crises, leftist authoritarian governments, right-wing authoritarian governments, men who can't commit, secret second families, and infighting of all kinds. But only the Central Americans have the disease doctors can't crack.

The disease isn't deadly. No one has died from it yet, even with reported complications related to vomiting and intestinal instability. Dehydration hasn't taken a single life. That in itself is a miracle, a doctor says on Telemundo in an attempt to assuage the quickly spreading fear. But a lot of people are sick, and a lot of people are missing work. Cities have begun crumbling: shrubs are overgrown, dishes unwashed, and diapers unchanged. The maids and landscapers and truck drivers are stuck in uncomfortable hospital beds. Call and call, their employers can't get a hold of them at their home numbers. That's why some white people are paying attention. Some are even demanding a cure, donating their hard-earned dollars to find treatments for the disease that appears to be the work of Lucifer or Christ, depending on who you ask.

Projections say that soon all the Guatemalans will have the disease, and soon all the Nicaraguans will, and eventually the Costa Ricans, until all the guanacos and catrachos are bedridden, their bodies hijacked by an ailment without a cure. It is not a full-blown apocalypse yet—there aren't enough people paying attention. The Central Americans are, but that's because it's tio and tia and abuelita who've been taken to the hospital, many against claims that they're fine and that the stomach bug will pass. (And also because they don't have health care.) But lots of other people are not paying attention, even when service seems slow at the restaurants and shopping centers they frequent. The *New York Times* is publishing an article about the disease next week, so maybe it'll be a full-blown, hold-your-children-close sort of crisis soon.

There's no need to panic, though. There's a lot of people to do that work. Some will even do it for the same under-the-table wages—paid in cash, off the books—that the Central Americans did it for before the plague swept in. Immigrants from Africa and Asia are looking for jobs. Other Latino laborers are looking for work too, so employers aren't too worried. Art galleries, nightclubs, and three-dollar-sign Yelp restaurants will be functioning to max efficiency in no time. This is just a temporary slowdown, a malfunction in the system.

The world looked, for just a moment, like it was going to fall apart because all the Salvadorans were sick. Whether or not doctors find a cure, the world will soon lift itself up and return to normalcy. It's not a pandemic, and all signs say it won't become one soon, which means the globe will keep on spinning with everyone in their rightful place.

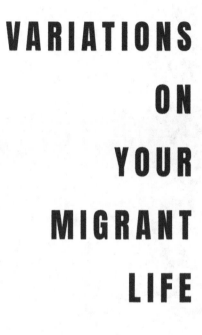

VARIATIONS
ON
YOUR
MIGRANT
LIFE

T'S STRANGE. USUALLY THE WORKDAY STARTS at dawn, even when you're only seven years old. There are chores to be done before breakfast. Mami makes a batch of fresh tortillas. Papi heads out to the grazing fields to feed the cows. A new brood of chicks was born last week, and it's been your job to put their crate outside in the morning. Today, though, no one woke you up.

You rub away eye-boogers and place a foot lightly on the dirt floor. The ground is compact and dust-free underneath your soles. A rooster crows outside. The room slowly comes into focus. Your adobe home has one window. It's a small cutout in the wall of dried bricks that solidified decades ago, before the war, before you were born. The early dawn light doesn't come from the window, but from the front door, which someone's left open in a rush.

Your hand moves back the thin, translucent curtain that separates your mattress from your parents' bed. The strewn sheets form impressions of the bodies that lay there the night before. Just outside, you hear low mutters and familiar footsteps, but they soon disappear. The patter of shoes on dewy earth whispers into silence. The home feels empty, and after a few minutes of silence, you can confirm it. You're alone.

IF IT'S BECAUSE MAMI LEFT, TURN TO PAGE 000.

IF IT'S BECAUSE PAPI LEFT, TURN TO PAGE 000.

Out under the spidery branches of the mamon tree, Papi explains that Mami has left for the United States. A couple of young men from the cantón work in places called Virginia and Indiana, but you've never heard of anyone's mother leaving. Mami is going to find work cleaning houses in California, Papi says. She'll send money back to help us, and hopefully she won't have to be gone for long.

Why did Mami leave instead of you? you ask. It's not like Papi leaving would have been better. You wish you could've told Mami goodbye before she left in the still of morning. The backs of your eyes burn. Tears form, but you force them down.

Papi says not to worry. As a distraction, he asks if you want to help retrieve the cattle from the pasture. The cows slurp loudly with their pinkish beige tongues when they drink out of the concrete well. It usually makes you laugh, so you agree to help.

In the next few months, you find ways of adjusting to life without Mami. The lady who lives by the highway sells Diana-brand snacks and cellular data cards from her front door. Papi hands you a couple crumpled dollar bills and sends you to the store. Mami communicates through WhatsApp. Her lilting tone crawls up the walls of the house when you hit play on a voice message. Sometimes you both have access to internet at the same time and you video-chat. Mami's face shatters into a kaleidoscope of pixels, the lag distorting her face.

I miss you. We'll be reunited soon, Mami says.

I believe you, you say.

Papi has always been a bit of a grump, with a stoic face and creases in his forehead he claims he's had since he was a teenager. He misses Mami, you can tell, but he doesn't show it. A woman starts coming around, younger than Mami and not as pretty. Her face is oval like an egg. Papi asks you not to tell Mami anything, and you don't. It'd be easy to tell her, but it wouldn't bring her back, so you remain quiet.

Things get harder. Mami's living expenses increase, and she sends less money home than Papi expected. At home, Papi struggles, burning the rice and serving undercooked beans. A couple of times, the young woman offers to cook, but you refuse to eat anything she's made. Meals become simpler. Smaller. Cheaper.

You call Mami on WhatsApp, and she talks to you only for a minute before asking to speak with Papi. He tells you to go outside and gather the gangly teenage chickens. When you come back, the creases on Papi's forehead have deepened. There are job opportunities for him in the United States with Mami. He can work as a fry cook or construction worker or landscaper. With those wages, he can buy you a new phone. They'll be able to support you better, even if from afar.

IF YOU BEG HIM TO STAY, GO TO PAGE 000.

IF YOU NOD AND TELL HIM YOU'LL MISS HIM, GO TO PAGE 000.

Crying is weakness. Papi's been clear about that. You try to harden your face, but heat flushes your cheeks. Scrunching your eyes doesn't help. Tears well up anyway.

Papi can't become just a voice on the phone or a crackling portrait of himself on the tiny phone screen. He can't go the same way Mami did. You sob. Your shoulder shakes. You beg Papi to stay. Please stay, please stay. Dried tears leave a salty film on your cheeks.

He doesn't leave for the United States.

The young woman with the egg head continues coming around. When she's there, Papi sends you outside. Sometimes you play with the plastic soccer ball the woman brought you as a peace offering. Sometimes you gather the chicks that run loose around the farm, scooping them into a crate so a stray dog doesn't gobble them up. But most often you stand underneath the single window and listen to the grunting and shuffling of sheets that you hear inside. Papi stayed for you, but maybe he stayed for this woman too.

Details about Mami are fading: the imprint of her fingers on the tortillas she tosses, the way her hair clumps together after a shower, the smell of the comal perfuming her skin as you hug her. You can't feel or smell or touch Mami over the phone. She can't hold you after a nightmare or sling a wet rag over your shoulders on a hot day. Soon she's been gone a year.

August marks the first harvest of the season. Verdant green stalks of corn bend down toward you, shuffling as you step through the gridded plot of land. Sun shines through the top of the stalks, casting a delicate pattern of shadows on your sun-burned skin. Last year the plot felt like an endless expanse of corn, but now you can see where the crop ends. You've gotten taller in the last year, yes, but the stalks haven't grown as high.

Some ears are kept for making atol de elote and masa at home, but most are sold for whatever profit Papi can strangle out of the disappointing harvest.

The soil is bad this year, Papi tells Mami on the phone. Though her words are muffled, you sense annoyance in her hurried sentences, loud outbursts, and long pauses. The land has been overcultivated, Papi explains, and with the climate, it hasn't produced like we wanted. Plus, those muchachos with their awful tattoos keep asking that we pay to sell at the market in San Vicente. It's going to be a hard year.

He complains about it to the young woman too, who pats him on the back and tells him it'll be okay. She does what Mami cannot.

Mami's cleaning jobs aren't enough. Hunger balloons in your gut. Papi struggles to buy seeds and fertilizer for the next season's harvest. He says he's run out of options. If he makes it to the United States, he can cobble together enough to build you a life. But you're too young, and the journey is too expensive, so he'd have to go alone. You grab on to his bicep, certain he'll float away if you don't.

IF YOU ASK HIM TO STAY AGAIN, TURN TO PAGE 000.

IF YOU STAY SILENT, TURN TO PAGE 000.

Hunger is an unbearable, inescapable weight. And still, your body feels so light.

When funds run low, you sell or eat the remaining livestock. Family members and neighbors bring what they can. Shyly, they hand over small portions of bread or a chicken here and there. The visitors wish they had more to offer, but hard times don't discriminate. There's little to go around.

Since infancy, you've had nimble legs as slender as a deer's. Thin, but healthy. The fragile line between slim and malnourished dissolves, and soon it's difficult to move around the world as you used to. Skin stretches between your ribs, and the bones protrude more than ever. The ache in your stomach is so consistent that it dulls into you, as if part of your anatomy.

Eventually all you can manage is the walk from your bed to the hammock on the front porch. The synthetic threads press against your skin as you lie looking up at the wood beams and ceramic shingles that make the roof. The ground has felt the pulse of departing footsteps. The front door became a portal. The porch separated what life had been and what it would become. A parent became memory here. Their touch transformed into a voice calling from far away.

When your gut swells and the fatigue sets in, the hunger becomes insurmountable. As you lay dying, your eyes shutter and all you have are snapshots of the farm around you. The light at dawn still pierces when a window or door is opened. The rooster's crow is still familiar and sharp. The smell of dirt is layered and complex. A hand rubs your back, and you hear soft crying, but still the weight is warm against your skin. In your last moments, you're not alone.

THE END.

TO IMAGINE ANOTHER LIFE FOR YOURSELF, TURN BACK TO PAGE 000.

TO MOVE ON TO THE NEXT STORY, FLIP
FORWARD TO PAGE 000.

With your nose pressed against Mami's clavicle, you cry quietly as she explains that Papi is looking for work in the United States. A coyote will make sure he makes it there safely, and once he pays off the debt from the journey, he'll send back money. Around you, the farm continues moving as it always has. Chickens peck at the dirt, shiny green leaves shake in the wind, and stray dogs wander the property's perimeter. But Papi is far away, and you don't know when you'll see him again.

When it's time for the harvest, Mami is forced to ask your tios—Papi's brothers—for help. She can manage the chickens and making fresh cheese, but she can't guarantee a successful harvest on her own. Your tios agree to help, though even among family favors come at a price. Mami agrees to give them a portion of the profits for their work. It's not much, but it's the most she can afford.

Papi was a man of actions, not words. He'd head to the fields before dawn, return at lunch, and then leave again until dusk. Whenever he was around, he offered you his spare minutes. At lunch, he'd cut a slice off his chicken breast and slide it onto your plate. In the evening, he peeled mamones and plopped them into your palm. He listened to you recount what you'd seen on television or read at school. Sometimes he'd tell the story of how he chased down his childhood bully with a slingshot, miming each dramatic twist.

Papi's grunts and huffs become faint the longer he's gone. His voice filers through the choppy static of the internet, and soon you can't remember the untarnished tone of his words. Now, when you miss him, you imagine him picking you up in his arms and twirling you, even though he never did that even when was around. You'd stare into his eyes, large and round like pebbles, and notice that they're the same shape and hue as yours.

Six months pass, then a year. Life is manageable, until you overhear Papi yelling on a phone call, a few weeks after the harvest. Your tios have siphoned more of the profits than they said they would. But Papi is so far away, so far north. There's nothing he can do but fume.

The longer Papi is gone, the smaller and smaller the benefits seem. The money from the corn harvest is less than it is most years. The remittances Papi sends make up for it, and there's a bit more to go around than there would be if hadn't left, but it doesn't seem worth the loss of your father. You pretend he's off in the fields and feel drips of disappointment when he doesn't return for lunch or dinner.

One day, Mami admits that she is thinking of joining him. He's saved enough to pay a coyote to take her across the border.

Your father is acting strange, she says. I think he's lonely.

She doesn't want to leave you here, but Papi can't afford passage for you both. Plus, two incomes will speed up the reunion.

If I leave, Mami says, we'll send for you soon.

Please don't leave me, you cry. You reach for her waist, and free your tears. Papi has already abandoned you, and you can't imagine Mami having to as well.

IF YOU ASK HER TO STAY, TURN TO PAGE 000.

IF YOU TELL HER YOU UNDERSTAND, TURN TO PAGE 000.

You search Mami's eyes, trying to figure out why she's decided to stay, but they give nothing away. That night, you lie together in a hammock that is almost too small for two. Mami holds you in the crook of her arm until you fall asleep.

When Papi calls next, his arm is in a cast. The cloth swaddles his arm from elbow to thumb. At his new construction job, his crew was asked to work on a rickety bit of scaffolding. A bar gave out, and Papi hit the ground, fracturing his wrist. When he complained to his employer, they said there was nothing they could do. If he goes to the authorities, they reminded him, he risks deportation. He doesn't have papers.

I'll figure it out, mijo, he says. He forces a smile, making his forehead wrinkles dance.

I believe you, you say. It seems easier for him to simply return, but you don't ask him to. He asks for Mami, so you hand the phone over and sneak outside, listening to the conversation through the window where she can't see you.

I love him too much to leave, Mami says.

The truest act of love would be offering him more from life, Papi argues. Even if it means leaving him behind for a bit.

Papi manages to find a job washing dishes, but the wages are much lower. Money becomes tighter, and Mami has no choice but to start selling off livestock. Mami has a favorite cow with a golden tuft of hair on its forehead. She named her Candy Candy, after the main character in her favorite cartoon from childhood, but eventually even Candy Candy will have to be sold. The money will run out soon.

When food gets harder to come by and Mami can't buy everything she wants to, she still finds a way to joke. Serving you a plate of beans and hand-thrown tortillas, she talks about her childhood. The last time I had this hard a time buying a bag of beans, she says, there was a war raging outside these walls. She laughs. But I survived that, so we'll make it through this, mi amor.

You do, until Papi admits his betrayal. He's been seeing a woman neither you nor Mami knew about. Mami shouts into her cell phone, calling him un sucio, un desgraciado, un hijueputa. He begs that she forgive him, and claims he's made a mistake. Join me, he says. We can work out our problems in person. She hangs up on him.

Papi's betrayal lights a fire under Mami, and she takes up a fight with your tios with a new vigor. In her eyes, you imagine, their faces become Papi's. Their thin faces morph to fill out his wider jaw and hairless face. She demands the money they've been withholding, and they pivot from evading accusations to simply denying them. You're stealing from your family, she says. Your own flesh and blood. What kind of men are you? Their faces remain stone-cold, though their eyes confess that they register Mami's anger.

One day, as you return from a visit to the lady who sells cellular data cards by the highway, you find a calf off the side of the dirt road. It looks dead. Bones jut from the matted bunch of tan fur on its back. It's still as a rock. But then you see its eyes, two dark orbs staring at you. Despite their alien size and unending depth, there's life in them. The calf, breathing shallowly, has surely been abandoned by its owner.

IF YOU TRY TO BRING THE CALF HOME WITH YOU, TURN TO PAGE 000.

IF YOU DECIDE THE CALF IS A LOST CAUSE, TURN TO PAGE 000.

You haven't eaten in hours, but you approach the calf anyway. It makes a small noise, somewhere between fear and gratitude. You try scooping the calf up in your arms, but even in its weakened state the animal is too heavy. The calf will have to walk down the dusty road on its own. Cupping your hands together, you hold the calf's head up and try bringing it to its feet. After a couple of attempts, it stretches its twiggy limbs to stand. Slowly, meter by meter, you make it back home.

She doesn't look great, Mami says. It'll take a lot for that calf to survive.

To start, you try to get her to suckle from Candy Candy, who is newly for sale. She rejects the calf and trots away whenever she approaches. You feed the calf by hand, but food is sparse, so you resort to theft. When your uncles are out attending to their crops, you sneak into their storage sheds and fill a bag with handfuls of feed. The calf's sinewy tongue licks it off your palm. With that, and whatever milk you and Mami can spare, the calf's body begins to fill out. She grows and grows, and soon it's clear she'll live.

The calf becomes a cow, and a healthy one. She gives birth to another calf and begins producing milk, more than any cow your family has ever owned. It's like a fountain. A fountain of youth, hopefully, Mami says with a laugh. She makes and sells more milk, more cheese. Candy Candy is no longer for sale. New calves are born. When Mami began selling off livestock as a last-ditch effort, the farm felt empty. But now it's hard to remember that emptiness. Cows butt heads as they fight to drink out of the concrete well. Goats bleat, and a whole choir of roosters mark the start of the day.

Your parents try working things out, but now there's more than just geography between you. You're taller now, older. If you were the tether holding Papi to San Vicente, you've stretched thin as he's pulled farther away. He sends less money. The money never stops completely, but it does wither. Mami doesn't admit it outright, but you see it in the lines carved like creeks in her face.

Eventually you remember the season Papi left, sometime in late summer, but forget the exact day or month. He calls and asks to speak to you every so often. Shrieks and cries, like the ones you made years ago, interrupt one of your calls. He sends money occasionally, but it feels symbolic now. You and Mami don't rely on it. Your tios keep taking a cut of the harvest, but it doesn't hurt as deeply anymore.

They can take it up with God, Mami says.

Who? you ask.

All those men, Mami says.

You're building a life, and it will be tenuous one, but your adobe home does not feel like a cage to escape. At night, you stare up at the endless expanse of stars that'll watch over you and Mami for years to come.

THE END.

TO IMAGINE ANOTHER POSSIBILITY FOR YOURSELF, TURN BACK TO PAGE 000.

TO MOVE ON TO THE NEXT STORY, FLIP FORWARD TO PAGE 000.

Even on the dirt road, you can picture where the beans and masa sit in your kitchen. They're stored in burlap sacks that have only been half-full, at most, in the past few months. The cattle Mami hasn't sold yet eat all the feed and their milk doesn't go far. There's no guarantee the calf will survive, but whatever it eats won't make it into your or Mami's mouths. On two skinny legs, you head home. You're hungry. Hopefully Mami has cobbled something together for lunch.

Beans and tortillas are waiting for you—an unextraordinary meal, but a meal nonetheless. Mami doesn't eat. She sits in silence for a while, very unlike herself. When she does speak, her words come out slowly, as if it hurts to say them. That morning, she received a message from a woman who used to live down the road, but now lives in Pomona, the city Papi left for. Papi has a secret Facebook account, one where he posts about his new life.

Mami slides her phone toward you. A crack runs across the screen, superimposed on the round cheeks of a young woman. Her eyes are a deep brown, her skin a softer tanned color. Without having to ask, you know you've glimpsed a photo of Papi's new woman.

This picture widens the chasm between you and Papi. The money he sends becomes less and less, even after Mami tells you that he's managed to snag a factory job that pays more than his dishwashing gig. Papi doesn't tell her about that new job. Information comes secondhand, until it doesn't come from him at all. Silence sets in, and the money dries out too.

Mami begins to skip meals, ensuring her portions end up on your plate. Abuelita brings a couple of tomatoes for you, but it's not much. Her garden is primarily for beautiful, inedible plants. Things get so dire that even your tios are struck by temporary guilt. They bring you some beans and plucked chickens.

It's ridiculous, Mami says after they drop off some food. They continue to rip us off and hope a few handfuls of beans make up for it. You agree, especially on the days when food is scarce and your gut aches like you've been punched hard.

On one such day, about three months after you last heard from Papi, you lie in the hammock on the front porch, avoiding anything that might worsen your fatigue.

We can't live life just hoping there'll be enough food for us, Mami says as she looms over you. Your good-for-nothing Papi wants me to join him in the United States. He says he's been saving money to pay a coyote to take me. He says he wants me back, that he regrets what he's done. He wants us to be a family again.

You sit up as much as you can in the threaded cocoon of the hammock. Mami's eyes become teardrops, and she stares back at you without certainty.

How big is Papi's home? you ask. Is there room for me there?

Your mother's face is stone-cold. If she knows the answer, she doesn't say it.

IF YOU TELL MAMI SHE SHOULD STAY, TURN TO PAGE 000.

IF YOU TELL MAMI SHE SHOULD GO, TURN TO PAGE 000.

Abuelita's house is across the highway and three miles into the sloping hills where cattle graze free-range. The dirt paths meander like the tunnels of an ant farm. They're especially dusty in the months when rain is scarce. Small flurries of dust collect around your ankles, as if you're walking through a parade of clouds.

Abuelita is Papi's mother, but she's lived alone for nearly a decade. She meticulously grooms the garden behind her home. It's full of flowers and plants pruned solely for their beauty, though there are a couple tomato stalks.

A few days after you arrive, Abuelita is hunched over, pulling weeds. You wander by, wanting to help, but she doesn't let you. She has few rules, but the most important is that you stay out of her garden.

It's okay, she says, go back inside. I'll be in to make lunch soon.

You don't hear from Mami or Papi for a month. As you lounge around your new home, you imagine the different ways your parents might have made their way north. Papi could have walked the entire way, the soles of his shoes regenerating like a snakeskin. Maybe Mami jumped on buses with cushioned seats and slept until she reached the border. They might have found a pool of water somewhere on the trip, jumped into it to refresh, and found themselves transported onto a quiet road with American houses in an American city in an American state.

Your parents finally call, and you try not to cry as Mami's voice cuts in and out. They're on speakerphone.

Mijo, she says, we live in an apartment. We'll buy you a bed when you arrive.

I miss you, bicho, Papi says. We'll work hard to bring you here.

Mami and Papi tell you more about the life you'll have one day. The city is called Pomona, and their apartment is by a highway with four roaring lanes. They say nothing about their journeys or their reunion. Despite the million questions you have, you stay mostly silent.

Finally, you ask: When can I join you?

Soon, mijo, Papi says. Soon.

Birthdays go by. Life is quiet for the most part, and you try connecting with your parents as much as possible over WhatsApp. They send money back to you and Abuelita, which she spends at the market in downtown San Vicente, always haggling for the best deal. When the price is right, she cooks towers of platanos fritos or spends entire afternoons simmering chicken soup. If you catch her in a good mood, she buys you strips of candied coconut. I like those a lot too, she admits with a smile.

On your tenth birthday, you video-call Mami and she holds up a pair of Nikes she's bought you. Silently, you hope they'll still fit once you get the chance to slip them on your small, callused feet. You're curious what her apartment looks like, and whether it has a massive couch like the ones in the movies, but she holds the phone close to her face.

One morning, a few days after you see the shoes, Abuelita is off visiting a neighbor. Someone shouts out your name. It's a boy's voice, but an unfamiliar one. A second of hesitation sets in, but you head outside. Three boys stand in Abuelita's garden, their white shirts clean and tight on their bodies. They're all a couple years older than you, but one stands in front—the clear leader.

We've been watching you, he says before plucking a cherry tomato from the vine and popping it into his mouth. The juice drip down onto his white ribbed-tank top. Shadows cover his arms, even as his shirt reflects the sun's brightness. He wipes the corner of his mouth and continues speaking.

We think it's time you join us. You can join our family, and we'll make sure you and your abuela stay safe. Understand?

The boy moves a hand to his hip, flashing the butt of a gun against his waistband. The shadows on his tanned skin are actually tattoos. Sweat drips down your cheek as you stare back at the boys in Abuelita's garden, considering their promises, digesting their threats.

IF YOU JOIN THE GANG, TURN TO PAGE 000.

IF YOU REFUSE, TURN TO PAGE 000.

The next time the boys come around, Abuelita is hunched over her garden, pulling out crushed seedlings and split vines. They wave. You wave back, but then hurry inside. Not to avoid them, but to sidestep Abuelita's questions.

Muchachos, she yells as they come up to the gate that separates the farm from the road. Get out of here! We don't need your bayuncadas. Malcriados!

The boys turn to leave, but it's only because of your agreement. Unlike many people in the cantón, she isn't scared of the gang members. Other people simply call them "los muchachos." It's a way of talking about a thing without giving it the power of a name. But Abuelita, she's fierce and she's old, so she thinks she's safe. You're not so sure. Abuelita continues to curse at them.

Los muchachos pop up again the next day. Abuelita isn't around, so you head down the road behind them. The trees droop down as you duck under some barbed wire, stepping off the main road and into Don Francisco's plot of land. Usually cows graze there in the afternoon, but today it's empty.

Take your shirt off, the leader says. You do, setting it gently on the ground. Before you've straightened out your body, he pushes you to the ground. Dirt burns your eyes, and the scratchy patch of grass irritates your skin. The boys pummel you in a flurry of shoes, fists, arms, legs. You count in your head. One, two three . . . The butt of a gun splits your skin open, and though your eyes are shut, you feel the burning trickle of blood down your temple. Four, five, six . . . A foot stomps hard on your ankle, sending a searing pain up your leg. Seven, eight, nine . . . The bruises will form by morning. Ten, eleven, twelve . . . Three boys feel like a dozen. At thirteen, the boys stop. You've been initiated.

One of the boys extends a hand to you, which you take. He pulls you in for a hug, wiping the dirt from your shoulder as he holds you. His chest is warm against yours. Let's go, he says. All the boys follow. You match their stride.

You spend the rest of the evening in a home that's new to you. The walls are made of cinder block and the roof is corrugated metal. A toddler, someone's younger brother, is watching *Peter Pan*. On-screen, small cartoon boys run around dressed up as forest animals, wielding wooden weapons. Together, they march across their island, whistling and singing. The Lost Boys. The bunch of you lounge around the home, half watching the film, messing around the way kids do.

Don't tell your abuela about what we're doing, the leader tells you as he walks you back to her farm. Stick with us. We're family now.

IF YOU TELL ABUELITA NOTHING AND CONTINUE SEEING THE BOYS, TURN TO PAGE 000.

IF YOU REGRET YOUR CHOICES AND DECIDE TO TELL ABUELITA WHAT'S HAPPENED, TURN TO PAGE 000.

Keeping the secret from Abuelita isn't too difficult, and soon you fall into a routine with the Lost Boys. At the cinder-block home, you eat meals of beans and rice, and sometimes a chicken leg or wing. Hitching rides in people's truck beds, you all go down to the market in San Vicente. The others go up to the vendors, asking for what they're due, while you stand watch. Eventually this'll be your job: asking for a fee in exchange for protection. You haven't seen anyone refuse, but one day you will. Hopefully, another person is sent to deal with it.

Mami and Papi have been sending Abuelita money, but the Lost Boys offer petty cash just for you. You buy Diana candies and chips, charamuscas from the woman down the street, and eventually a pair of shoes when yours are worn. The Nikes from California never arrived. If Abuelita notices the small treasures that appear in the home, she doesn't point them out. After a couple of weeks, you've become a Lost Boy.

To make it public, a boy takes a needle to your collarbone, staining your skin with dark ink. The design is simple, just two letters: MS. Your collarbone is irritated for a while, but when the red softens, the tattoo is sleek and stunning against your skin. The boys promise you more tattoos soon, and it's easy to imagine a whole sleeve blooming like flowers all over your body.

When you get home, Abuelita panics.

I'm calling your parents, she says. I can't believe you've let yourself get caught up in those muchachos' bullshit.

Mami and Papi call back the next day. Asking for favors wasn't easy, but they've borrowed enough money to bring you to the United States. You feel a tinge of melancholy at the thought of leaving. It outweighs any reunion you imagine with your parents, whose faces have become wrinkled in your head. They don't understand the life you've built for yourself in their absence.

You won't go. You'll never again live in the adobe home

where you born, and you won't feel small in your parents' arms as they hold you close. You're too tall. They're too far. It's bearable, though, because you won't be forced to leave your cozy patch of the country. You have friends here. Brothers. You'll make a life here. You've found where you belong.

THE END.

TO IMAGINE ANOTHER POSSIBILITY FOR YOURSELF, TURN BACK TO PAGE 000.

TO MOVE ON TO THE NEXT STORY, FLIP FORWARD TO PAGE 000.

When you tell Abuelita about the boys, she takes the news quietly, though her mouth tenses and a glint of worry crosses her eyes.

Don't leave the house, she says. We're going to keep the doors closed, especially when I'm away.

The walls are sturdy and impenetrable. Midday, a bit of light makes its way through a piece of the roof patched with corn husks. Most of the time, though, you shuffle through the house in darkness. Sometimes there are muffled shouts outside. It's Abuelita arguing with someone, her voice as fearless as ever. This is what you love most about her: she sticks around to fight for you.

This goes on for about two weeks, until Abuelita comes in with pink scrapes on her forearms.

They threw rocks at me, she says. I covered my face, but the rocks scratched up my arms.

It's all my fault, you think. Youth is a resource and a curse. If you weren't around, los muchachos would leave Abuelita alone. For a split second you consider climbing into the trees and never coming down, but that won't work either. Another goodbye would be too much to bear.

Down the street, a boy is killed. Rumors say he was being recruited into the gang and refused. When he was on his way back from feeding his families' cattle, a marero put a bullet into his chest. His body lay in the sun for a couple of hours, his blood dyeing the scattered feed a deep crimson.

When Mami and Papi hear this, they drain their meager savings and borrow money from a friend to pay a coyote to bring you to them. They wanted more stability before bringing you over, Abuelita explains, but plans change.

The night before you leave, Abuelita moves around in a whirl preparing for your journey. She cooks tortillas and wraps them in a cloth towelette, packing them beside the avocados already in your backpack. She embroiders a phone number into a T-shirt, folds it, and zips the bag shut.

The coyote will be here in a few hours, and you're going to try to get some sleep, so it's finally time to say goodbye to Abuelita. With you gone, the boys will leave her alone. You hope. The ache of leaving mixes with the prospect of seeing your parents.

IF YOU SPEND A LONG TIME SAYING GOODBYE, TURN TO PAGE 000.

IF YOU SAY GOOD NIGHT AND GOODBYE QUICKLY, TURN TO PAGE 000.

Before the roosters have clucked, Abuelita walks you to the side of the highway. A shadow approaches and, squinting your eyes, you make out a swollen belly and a baseball cap. The coyote is shorter than you had assumed, and older, likely in his midforties. His cheeks are full, his beard patchy. He doesn't introduce himself. He simply says that he'll be guiding you to the United States. As he speaks into his cell phone, his voice is high and airy. The coyote doesn't strike you as the sort of man who'd protect you in a crisis.

A few minutes later, a pickup truck arrives. The coyote grabs you by the armpits and hoists you into the truck bed. As the sun begins to rise, Abuelita becomes a dot in the distance. Shades of purple creep over everything. You wave goodbye.

The truck stops several times in the next two hours. The truck bed fills up. Soon you're accompanied by a man in his forties, two tattooed teenagers a few years older than you, and a woman and her swaddled infant. A stranger might confuse you for a family. The highway stretches in front of you, and trees bend toward the asphalt. Your country is not all that large, and soon the car approaches Guatemala.

The coyote slips a customs officer a wad of cash at the border, and he waves the truck along. The wheels spin and spin, stopping only once to pick up a boy who looks about your age, only chubbier. He's friendlier than you too. Minutes into the ride, he's already made friends with the infant in the woman's arms. They play peek-a-boo for nearly an hour.

It's late when you arrive in Guatemala City. The truck pulls up to a motel parking lot and your eyes begin to close. The next morning, you wake leaning against the hard plastic of the truck bed. It's nearly six in the morning, which means Abuelita will be pruning her tomato plants soon. Is she thinking of you too?

The Guatemalan boy is awake and has moved to sit next to you.

I'm Hugo, he says. You tell him your name and smile, glad to have a friend.

Another bribe gets you into southern Mexico, though this time on foot. The truck turns back toward San Salvador. We'll be less noticeable if we walk, the coyote says.

Your backpack gets lighter, and after a few days of walking, it's almost empty. You've eaten all the food Abuelita packed. Hugo offers you a bit of tortilla he has in his bag. You say thank you, and stay close to him after that.

The coyote deviates from any major roads and walks you through wild brush. Eventually the trees and bushes thin out to reveal railroad tracks. You sit and wait for hours. A small group of women join eventually. They hold plastic bags filled with bread, and hand you a bundle to split with Hugo.

The train is going to come quickly, the coyote explains. It'll be loud, but you can't hesitate. When people hesitate, they lose limbs. Get a running start before jumping. Most of the shipping containers have ladders. Hold on tight and pull yourself up.

A far-off rumble becomes deafening. A set of whistles signal the train's approach. It's monstrous and so much taller than you. As the shipping containers approach, the group of women swing their arms in circles and lob bread into the sky. The bags arc into the hands of men already sitting atop *La Bestia*. Ladders pass you by; the train isn't infinite. Most of your party has already gotten onboard. You and Hugo are the last ones left on the ground. The sun is bright and scalding. The train roars. Your legs shake. You're terrified.

IF YOU TAKE A DEEP BREATH, FORCE YOUR THIN LEGS TO RUN, AND REACH FOR THE MOVING LADDER, TURN TO PAGE 000.

IF FEAR PARALYZES YOU, TURN TO PAGE 000.

Your hand slams onto the rusty metal rung. Paint flakes scrape your palm. For a moment your feet hang limp in the air, lurching as the train whizzes down the tracks. It's hard to move without loosening your grip, but you manage to place a shoe on the ladder. It slips, but you cement your footing and climb up. Once you catch your breath, you look at the ladder expecting to see Hugo's head pop up behind you. When it doesn't, you crane your neck to see if he's sitting atop one of the train cars behind yours. He isn't there either.

You search for Hugo in the distance, either on the tracks or beside them, but the train is moving too quickly. The spot where you'd been standing flattens into the horizon. Frustrated, you throw a piece of bread, hoping it'll float through the air and find its way into Hugo's hands. The women must have taken him with them, you tell yourself, though you wish he was sitting next to you, atop the train where the wind is loud in your ears.

Riding *La Bestia* isn't pure salvation. Danger makes it another liminal space—treacherous, temporary, but unavoidable if you're ever going to reunite with your parents. Most migrants ride on top, holding on to whatever bit of metal they can. You dodge tree branches as they whip past you, but one strikes your arm and leaves red welts.

The wind is cold, relentless. You bundle yourself with the second shirt in your backpack, but still you shiver. If Abuela was there, she'd hold you close, sharing her body heat. Thieves jump onto the train, but the coyote pulls out a gun, so they keep their distance. Instead, the thieves approach a group of migrants a few cars away who journey without a guide.

After a dozen hours and two trains, the coyote urges your group to climb off as *La Bestia* temporarily slows. Remember what we talked about, he says. The authorities are looking for people like you, so pretend you're from here.

You run through what you learned on the train: the name

of the Mexican president, the Mexican words for straw and jacket, the Mexican national anthem, the name of your Mexican hometown, the name of your favorite Mexican soccer team. With your new identity, which you'll only reveal if forced, you venture farther into the Mexican state of Sonora.

The coyote makes scraggly back roads and small towns into a trail that ends at the edge of the desert. He hands you a water bottle and tells you to conserve it. The upcoming journey is treacherous and hot, but he knows the geography well and will guide you through the land where it'll offer the least resistance.

The trek starts in the early morning. It's already warm, but not insufferable. The soles of your shoes sink in spots where the sand is loose. As the sun rises in the sky, heat blankets everything. The young woman with the infant stops to latch the child onto her nipple, and the group slows down as she breastfeeds. She offers you a smile as you wait for her. Her cheeks are flushed red from the heat, and your lightheadedness means yours must be too.

A layer of sweat glosses your skin. Your eyes burn when the salt drips into your eyes, but you continue walking. The horizon is endless, and were it not for the coyote's constant reassurance, you'd be convinced that your legs have been taking you in endless circles.

The night is freezing and windy. Bits of sand whip your face as you try getting some sleep. The cycle continues: hot, cold, hot. Sand and sweat mix. More hours pass. As you approach the edge of the desert, the coyote forces you to stop more frequently. Quiet, he urges, I think I heard a noise. Could be the wheels of a border patrol truck.

Though you're unaware when it happens, your feet touch ground in the United States. The earth behind you is Mexico, the dirt ahead is America.

What choice do you have?

FOLLOW THE COYOTE AND TURN TO PAGE 000.

You freeze. If the train wasn't rushing past in a blur of rust and spray paint, you'd believe time had stopped. Hugo doesn't wait for you any longer. He runs along the track, stomping with each step, but eventually gaining speed. He grips a ladder, but as he tries to pull himself up, the speed of the train flails him about. He loses his hold and tumbles back onto the ground, hitting the edge of the tracks before rolling into the packed dirt.

You spring into action, finally, jogging to him. You crouch by his side. His arms are bloodied by deep scrapes, and most of his left side will be bruised by morning. His eyes are open, but he's out of breath. His cheeks are flushed, like two of Abuelita's tomatoes. The train gets smaller and smaller as the women who were throwing bread approach to help.

He's lucky, one says. I've seen people lose arms to the train with falls like that. The women offer you a meal and a place to sleep. They see you as you are: children simply trying to survive. Few see you that way anymore.

The women are a saving grace. They don't have money to offer but feed you for a few days. They're familiar with the plight of migrants, and they know you and Hugo won't turn back now, so they flag the dangers that lie ahead. Avoid policemen if you can, one woman says. They're looking for migrants and they won't let you go without a bribe. Tijuana isn't the best place to cross, but we might be able to help you get there. Just don't cross carrying marijuana for a narco. That never ends well.

A series of men in pickup trucks transport you northward. You and Hugo pretend to be siblings. The thought of him as your brother makes you both smile. If you get stopped by Mexican authorities, you'll say the driver is your father. Hugo talks the whole way. Unlike you, he loves going to church. He's an altar boy, and he already misses waking up early for Sunday morning mass. He doesn't have a mother. Or if he does, he doesn't mention her. His father lives in Iowa, where he slices poultry up for a living.

Is that near California? you ask.

I don't think so, Hugo says.

The drivers get you to a more northern city, and from there you and Hugo use your last remaining dollars to buy a bus ticket to Tijuana. As you wait at the bus terminal, you avoid eye contact with the armed policemen loitering around the entrance and by the storefronts across the street.

In Tijuana, Hugo tells you his father tried entering San Diego once. He was caught, and before being sent back to Guatemala, he spent time at a church that sheltered migrants. There's a good lesson there, Hugo says. When you're lost, you can always turn to the Lord. Sometimes Hugo talks like a man, even though he is a boy. If he's afraid of what's to come, he doesn't show it.

You ask around meekly, and manage to find a similar organization that takes you in for a few days. The people there are from all over—Honduras, Guatemala, Venezuela, Haiti, other parts of Mexico—and everyone seems to have their own rumors to share. One man says there are two ways to cross, though neither guarantees anything. You can present yourself at a port of entry to apply for asylum, or you can try finding a small corridor in the rocky dessert to cross the border by foot.

You decide to leave, but Hugo says he's staying at the shelter for another few days. His parents are going to take out a loan to pay for another coyote to guide him into the United States. Mami and Papi have spent too much money already and borrowed who knows how much.

I'm so glad we met, you tell Hugo.

I'll be praying for you, he says. You return the promise before hugging him goodbye.

IF YOU DECIDE TO TRY RECEIVING ASYLUM AT A

PORT OF ENTRY, TURN TO PAGE 000.

*IF YOU DECIDE TO CROSS INTO THE UNITED
STATES BY FOOT, TURN TO PAGE 000.*

Early in the morning, the director of the shelter drives you to the San Ysidro port of entry. He hands you a meal packaged in a Styrofoam container and points to the line where migrants wait to present themselves to uniformed American officers. Good luck, he says, before driving away.

As you wait in line, you rehearse what you'll say to the officer when he asks why you're applying for asylum. You'll tell him that Mami and Papi are in the United States. You'll talk about the gang, and how they came to harass you and Abuelita. You'll describe the fear you felt when you saw them, and how the sight of a gun sent a chill through you. You'll lay all your fears in front of the officer, like an animal dissected in a laboratory. I need to be with my parents, you'll say. I don't want to go to the United States, but I need to.

You never meet with an officer. The line moves slowly for a few hours, a few steps at a time, until it finally stops. An official comes by explaining that they're done hearing asylum pleas for the day. A woman in front of you cries out. I've been coming here for almost three weeks, and every day you people say the same shit! The same shit!

The official shrugs. Metering. It's policy, he says.

A crowd forms. A young man is speaking, quiet but commanding, like a priest delivering his homily. I know a way through the desert, he says. He says that people's loved ones can pay once they've made it through. Your other option is the shelter, but after that, an endless line awaits you. Even if you miraculously reach its end, you're not guaranteed asylum. Mami once said that sharks die if they stop moving, and that's exactly how you feel. This limbo you're in, alone in a country that isn't your own, is even scarier than the place you left.

THE DESERT IS YOUR ONLY CHOICE. TURN TO PAGE 000.

The next morning, you leave from a small town several miles from Tijuana. A stretch of hilly, rocky desert is rumored to be the spot with the lowest odds of encountering narcos or Border Patrol agents. The young man guides the group, ten who've chosen to trust him. The plan sounds simple enough: walk straight through the desert until you peep buildings reaching for the sky.

The sun is tyrannical as it blazes down. You've been walking for hours, leaving your skin flush and sunburned. The heat has penetrated even your organs, kindling for the slow burn spreading inside. Your body hurts. The spit in your throat has all but dried up, and your mouth matches the aridness of the desert.

Somehow, the young man has lost his way. An argument breaks out, but it goes nowhere. The only choice is to continue walking, so you do. You finish the only water bottle you've brought. You trip and twist your ankle, sending a sharp pain up your calf. Shake it off and continue walking, you tell yourself, even as a dull pain settles in.

Lightheaded, you sit on a rock for just a second. Out in the distance, a small pool of water appears. Focusing your eyes is difficult, so you stumble toward it, but it continues to get farther and farther away. You stop again, and sit on a different rock, but the mirage is still there. Out of its ripples, a person-shaped form rises. Another pops up beside it. It's Mami and Papi, out in the desert in front of you.

Your body hurts, but you run toward them, ignoring the pleas from the rest of the group. You slip, slamming your palms into hot sand to break your fall. Grains of sand coat your sweaty hands. You get up and run again. Mami, Papi, and the water move farther away. You run. It's hot and everything burns. Sweat gets into your eyes. Tears well. It's a miracle that there's any moisture left in your body at this point. You sit but struggle to stand up again. You stay there, crumpled over yourself, waiting.

You want to continue toward Mami and Papi, but the desert

is merciless. Despite your disorientation, you want to escape the desert's grip.

IF YOU HEAD TOWARD MAMI AND PAPI, TURN TO PAGE 000.

IF YOU STAY PUT, TURN TO PAGE 000.

You stumble toward your parents on the horizon, until you can't move any farther. Unable to gently lower yourself, you fall hard onto the ground. Mami and Papi are gone. There's no sight of water ahead, no liquid to deflect the sun's relentless smolder.

Lightheaded, you struggle to keep your eyes open. Desperately, as if it'll help, your eyes dart back and forth, absorbing whatever they land on. The branches of a young mesquite bush wave in the breeze. A lizard scurries out of sight. Rocks pop out of the sand like boils.

A few feet away, there's a pile of man-made objects. With all the energy you have left, you scoot toward it, but as you approach, the smell of piss assaults your nostrils. You can make out a backpack, a pair of jeans, rosary beads, food wrappers, and crushed canned goods. Much of the pile is charred. You reach out for a gallon container, but it's empty. A gash has been cut into the blue plastic.

The desert is hot, and you're hungry. You're losing grasp of what's real, and all you want to do is lie down in the sand. You feel warm all over, but the pain starts to dissipate. Instead, it's like you're bundled up in a blanket. All your muscles relax, and the last images that flit through your mind are your parents' faces. The details are blurry, and you're not sure how their voices really sound or how their calluses feel pressed against your cheek. You put together as accurate a memory as you can before closing your eyes for the last time.

THE END.

TO IMAGINE ANOTHER POSSIBILITY FOR YOURSELF, TURN BACK TO PAGE 000.

TO MOVE ON TO THE NEXT STORY, FLIP FORWARD TO PAGE 000.

Though you'd do anything to hold your parents tight, you can't muster the energy to move toward them. Instead, you close your eyes for a long time, trying to hide from the sun. The white shapes that dance around on your eyelids remind you that it's still blazing. When you open your eyes, the pool of water is gone. There's nothing but endless desert.

A light rumbling breaks through. The dryness in your mouth is so intense, the inside of your cheek might crack into shards. The noise gets louder, which might be a sign of madness. You're lightheaded. Between slow blinks, the rest of the group scatters, leaving you alone.

The sound stops, replaced by footsteps behind you. You crane your neck and see a man in a green uniform: heavy knee-high black boots, a military vest across his chest, a gun strapped to his side.

The Border Patrol agent drives you to a processing facility. It's a lifeless warehouse, like the kind used to store extra animal feed or a broken-down pickup truck in San Vicente. But once you enter, it's clear that the place is full of life, overcrowded even. Hundreds of migrants are waiting. You're starving, and all you get is a cold sandwich. Some people around you have toothbrushes and foil blankets, but you aren't offered any. The facility is freezing. Everyone is funneled into different sections of chain-link fencing—cages, really.

You keep to yourself, afraid of causing trouble. Some of the people around you look exhausted and dirty. Not everyone gets to shower every day, and many people have been in this facility for over a week. Eavesdropping, you hear one man say his cousin told him it's illegal to keep people in the processing facility longer than seventy-two hours.

Finally, after two nights of restless sleep, an agent pulls you from the crowd and takes you to be interviewed. An asylum officer asks you a set of questions. Some are easy: You're from San

Vicente in El Salvador. Some are difficult: How can you possibly describe the way it feels to have your life threatened by gang violence? Or how on some nights Mami and Papi's absence made your chest feel full of lead?

The asylum officer calls you lucky. Many people meet him, and many are forced to wait longer. Some asylum seekers are sent back to Mexico, some to ICE detention centers. People your age are sent to special children's centers. But you, you're a lucky one.

He doesn't verbalize it, but his body and tone make it abundantly clear: The system runs on the individual decisions of men like him. With that kind of power, you could have made Mami, Papi, and Abuelita stay. If your life hinged on your choices, there'd have been no desert to get lost in, no crossing to survive.

This man holds your trajectory in his supple white hands. And today he's decided to release you to your parents. Using the number Abuelita sewed into your shirt, the authorities contact your parents and organize your drop-off. In a few hours, you'll be in their arms again.

TURN TO PAGE 000.

By some miracle, almost everyone makes it: the two teenagers, the man who looks a bit older than your father was when he left, the woman and her baby, who has cried less than you'd expected her to.

You think of Hugo. Being alone must have been terrifying. A few split seconds, a couple of different decisions, and you could have been like him, stranded in unfamiliar land. Is he still in Mexico? Or did he join another group, a second fake family, that led him to Iowa? He must have made it, you tell yourself. In your mind, you see him. He's running free on a playground, then swinging across the monkey bars as his father watches, ready to catch him if he falls.

You spend the night in a studio apartment. The only piece of a furniture is a dusty brown couch, and the group agrees that the woman and her child should have it. You find a slice of scratchy carpet to sleep on, but at least it's not sand. The walls protect you from the cold, and you try to ignore the dirt in your shoes and in your scalp. You sleep, not fully at rest, but more deeply than you have in days.

The next morning, you and one of the teenagers get into a pickup truck driven by a stranger. He takes you onto a multi-lane highway. It's nearly three times as wide as the highway that runs through San Vicente. A couple of hours later, the truck pulls into a Walmart parking lot.

The air is dry. Around you, people step out of their cars and walk toward the storefront. No one pays attention to you, but you still feel ashamed that your shirt is so dirty. This isn't how your parents remember you, and this isn't the image you want them to have when they arrive. A car honks nearby, and the tattooed teenager walks toward it, offering only a slight wave goodbye.

You're readjusting your shirt by tucking it into your shorts, as if that will make the dust less noticeable, when a voice calls out your name. It's a warped version of the sound that emanated from Abuelita's cell phone. A second voice joins, another variation.

A few meters away—separated by asphalt, a couple of shiny cars, and the weight of years apart—your parents wave to you. You take one slow step forward, then another. Mami and Papi stay in place, as if the ardent Arizona sun has melded their rubber soles to the asphalt. When you get within arm's length, you stop. A hand reaches for you. It grazes your cheek, your jaw, the bottom lobe of your ear.

TRY NOT TO FLINCH. TURN TO PAGE 000.

The two-bedroom apartment becomes your first home in this country. You share it with your parents and hope that it'll eventually become more comfortable. It's nothing like the place your parents left, and nothing like Abuelita's home with the garden out back. The space inside is much smaller, and the surrounding landscape is a sprawling ecosystem of strip malls and concrete. A gray sheen covers everything except, on the clearest days, the vast blue sky.

Mami and Papi ask lots of questions, but none of the difficult ones. At the store, they wonder what your favorite color is. Is it blue or red or purple? At breakfast, they ask if you want your eggs scrambled or fried. Papi says: Pretty nice car, huh? Mami asks: Did you leave the television on last night?

You hold your own questions close to your chest. Why did you leave me for so long? Did you miss me? Is Abuelita okay? When are we going back to see her? Do you know how the Sonoran sun feels at midday? Can you still feel the grains of sands scraping your skin? Do you know the sort of hunger that makes you feel light enough to float away? Was it worth it, Mami and Papi? Is this all worth it?

Instead, you and your parents try slipping into the mundane as if there are no gaps, as if what you've been through has not created a chasm between you. It's a valley only you can see.

What do you want to eat? Mami asks.

To celebrate your first month here, we can go to a restaurant, Papi says.

A hamburger? you ask.

Of course, they say together.

Here, while Mami and Papi work during the day, you go to school. It's daily, unlike in San Vicente, where there was too much farmwork to walk to the schoolhouse every day. At first wrangling the English language proves difficult. Your teacher speaks Spanish, but she doesn't let you speak it in the classroom.

How do we say that in English? she asks, and you stumble after an answer.

Your mouth twists and contorts as your tongue maneuvers the rhythms and sounds of English. Tediously, painfully, you readjust your mouth to speak more fluidly. Some sounds still trip you up. Certain combinations of letters remain jagged at their edges. For a while your pronunciation worries your teacher, but eventually you speak without shame. Soon your English is clearer than Mami and Papi's, though you only hear theirs when they speak to your teacher or a telemarketer.

Still, as you learn the rules of this new country and your new life, you struggle to speak of what you've been through. It doesn't matter what language might be used or the inflections in which you'd recount the journey. Silence fills the apartment whenever Mami and Papi are around, as if it too, like the wall studs or concrete foundation, were integral to the structure of the building. Desperately, you want to break the silence. But desire and action are like nations split by a river. Bridging the gap proves treacherous.

The urge strikes you again when you return to the diner you went to during your first few weeks in Pomona. The booth's seats are still plasticky, and you order another hamburger with a side of fries. The questions dance on your tongue and your jaw unclenches slightly, ready to ask them how their journey was, whether they felt as aimless and desperate as you did. The words are tacky like the beef you grind between your teeth.

IF YOU BREAK THE SILENCE, TURN TO PAGE 000.

IF YOU DON'T, TURN TO PAGE 000.

Were you scared, you ask, when you came to the United States?

Papi stares down at his plate as if you haven't said anything at all. Mami stares back at you with sad eyes.

I was, she says. But it doesn't matter now. We're together, bicho.

They don't say anything else, but asking the question cracks something open. As you grow older, you find ways of bridging the gap between you and your parents. Meeting with a school psychologist helps. You're sent to her for what your teacher calls "inappropriate and disruptive behavior in the classroom." What really happened was that your friend, of which you have a handful now, was bugging you. He kept saying, You're Mexican, aren't you? and you said, No, I'm not. But he kept saying, Mexican, Mexican, over and over, and you got annoyed, so you hit him. It wasn't a hard punch, but he snitched, so you got sent to the psychologist.

The psychologist has long black hair and a round face. Her glasses are round and small, which gives her a funny look. She wasn't smiling when you arrived the first time, so you didn't laugh. She asked you to explain what happened, and why you reacted the way you did.

Where is your family from? she said.

El Salvador, you said. Immediately you remembered Mami and Papi told you not to tell people that.

You meet with the therapist regularly, and after the initial meeting, she's much warmer. She pushes you but doesn't prod when your hesitation is clear. You find yourself talking about memories you had squirreled away. You say, I lay in a hammock and cried out for my parents until I lost my voice. You say, The growl in my stomach sounded like an angry wildcat whenever I'd had less than enough to eat. You say, I still feel the heat of the sun in the Sonoran Desert on my scalp and underneath my thin rubber soles. You say, I went years without being able to talk to my parents in person and now I can't say a word. You say, I still dream of the roaring train and the ghosts created on the path we treaded.

Repetition makes the past bearable, though there is a dull pain that accompanies the first few retellings. After a while, what you've experienced becomes just another story about yourself that you tell. One day, which is otherwise ordinary, you're able to tell Mami and Papi about how the boys stood in Abuelita's garden eating her cherry tomatoes. You say that you were scared, and that you missed them extra that afternoon.

They share a memory—one that was a prickly, untouchable thing until recently—about their first weeks in this country. Mami and Papi were at a supermarket, one they'd never been to before, looking for a bag of masa. They could only find all-purpose flour, so they asked an employee. But the employee didn't speak Spanish, and instead of helping them, he laughed. A shrill, cruel snicker. They left the store without the masa, upset that they couldn't say or ask what they wanted to. And like that—together, story by story—you poke at the silence bit by bit until it tears. From that gap, you can slowly, painfully pull your family back together.

Life continues, and your new country debates whether your family deserves to remain as the unit it is. Mami and Papi tell you not to worry, but when they left you, it wasn't completely by choice. Plus, you've seen the reports on Univision. Your family could be forced apart again.

Who would you miss most, if you had to miss them again?

IF IT'S MAMI, TURN TO PAGE 000.

IF IT'S PAPI, TURN TO PAGE 000.

At the diner, you can't bring yourself to ask the question that burns the back of your throat, so you stare at the décor. There's a black-and-white photograph of the diner back in 1957 with a long retro Chrysler out front. An American flag hangs behind the cash register. Instead of asking your parents if they were scared when they made their way to the United States, you replay the facts you've learned about the flag in school. Thirteen stripes for thirteen colonies. Fifty stars for fifty states.

You've learned a lot of things at school: curse words, multiplication tables, and the comfort you find in new friendships even when you don't have language for it. You get into a disagreement with one of your friends when he doesn't stop insisting that you're Mexican like him, but you stop arguing when your teacher walks by.

At home, you've learned too: not to open the door to a stranger, to quiet your voice in public, that any stranger could uproot your entire family. Often Mami, Papi, and you will get close to talking about what you've been through. Every time a birthday passes—Papi's in April and Mami's in June—you think of all the birthdays you didn't spend together, all the gifts that never found you, all the loneliness you felt. At the last second, you avoid the conversation.

In the moment, it's easiest to relinquish yourself to the silence, letting it engulf you like a riptide. If you were to say something, if you were to allow your lips to loosen and to talk about how often you cried and how alone you felt in those years, you and your parents might hurt each other. Deep-burrowed resentment could burst into angry words; yelling unlike any you've done before, but that you know you're capable of. A fire that sits in the back of your throat.

So you say nothing. It seems easier. Instead, you hug Mami and hope your hands communicate the extent of your feeling. You sit on the couch near Papi after his first shift of the day is over and hope that's enough. Words remain thoughts, and the longer they do, the harder it is to penetrate the silence. It's the sort of quiet that will fester over time, that will seep into the person you grow into. It'll sit inside you until it flares up and does harm to others. But for now, and likely for years, your family leaves miles unsaid.

Life continues, and your new country debates whether your family deserves to remain as the unit it is. Mami and Papi tell you not to worry, but when they left you, it wasn't completely by choice. Plus, you've seen the reports on Univision. Your family could be forced apart again.

Who would you miss most, if you had to miss them again?

IF IT'S MAMI, TURN TO PAGE 000.

IF IT'S PAPI, TURN TO PAGE 000.

All the children stand outside the school's front gate, waiting for their parents. A teacher watches over the group until the last student is picked up. Mami's employers often want her to stay late to finish up a task they assigned last-minute. On those days, she apologizes but still shows up.

Today you're the only child left. Staring down at your Nikes, with your shoulders up to your ears, you try making yourself small so that cars driving by won't see that you're still waiting, which to them inevitably means that your parents love you less than the other children's parents love them. Your teacher stands next to you, but you have nothing to say to her. Still, she asks: Is your parent coming? And you respond, Yes, even though you're not sure.

When Mami finally arrives, her eyes are puffy and red. Her hair is always a bit disheveled when she picks you up, but today it's like she hasn't looked in a mirror at all. She hasn't even run a hand through it or anything. You walk toward Mami slowly, as she apologizes to the teacher for making her wait. If the teacher notices that something is wrong, she doesn't say it. She just nods and waves you both off.

When you get into the car, Mami puts the key in the ignition but doesn't move for a long time. The soft rumble of the car is the only noise, until Mami finally explains what happened.

I was driving to get you, she says. My patrona wanted me to stay another twenty minutes to watch her daughter while she took a quick shower. I stayed, and then got into the car and hurried to get here. And I didn't even notice, but a police officer stopped me and told me I was going over the speed limit. I swear I wasn't, and if I was, it could not have been much over. But he stopped me and I started thinking about Señora Tita, who got deported after she accidentally missed a stop sign. I started crying and crying, thinking about her. But the police officer let me off with a warning. He drove away, but I stayed there shaking for a long time.

You reach out and squeeze Mami's hand, but don't let your fingers linger. After a few more seconds, she puts her hands on the steering wheel.

Let's go home, you say.

TURN TO PAGE 000.

In many ways your life is like any other child's. You go to school, join a soccer team, and spend afternoons complaining about your homework. But you and your parents live with more caution than those around you, which makes the occasional arguments between your parents feel strangely normal, like the ones you see on sitcoms and soap operas on TV.

The latest fight happens in the kitchen. You're sitting at the kitchen table, shoveling shredded chicken and rice into your mouth, when Papi walks in and says he's been fired.

It wasn't my fault, he says. My boss is an asshole.

It's never your fault, Mami responds. Nothing is ever your fault.

He fired me because he didn't like me, Papi says. I didn't do anything wrong.

Their voices escalate until Mami resigns herself and goes into their bedroom. The bags under Papi's eyes are deep, deeper than you remember them being back in San Vicente.

Don't eat so messily, Papi says, pointing to the grains of rice that have fallen off your plate. He doesn't say anything else before moving to the living room, where he sits in front of the TV as it drones on. The next few weeks are different, as Papi lounges around the house and takes over the task of picking you up from school. Meals get a bit simpler too—lots of beans, lots of pasta—but there's still enough to eat. Eventually Papi gets a different job, and though it doesn't pay as well, it brings peace back into the apartment.

A few days after he starts his new job, Papi sits in front of the TV quietly. You sit next to him and pretend to fill out a worksheet, though really all you're doing is doodling in the margins.

Mijo, he says gesturing to your homework, it's important that you work hard in school. It gives you opportunities. You can go to college, get a degree, and then get a nice job so you don't have to work outdoors like me. Keep your skin free of sunburns and calluses. Never have to work jobs that break your body, like the one I lost. Though, you know, it's sort of a blessing I got fired.

You look at him quizzically, and he looks back at you, realizing he revealed more than you knew. He nods and continues.

The boss didn't like me, for some reason. Said I was stubborn because I asked questions when he tried changing up my responsibilities. But we're lucky. A few days ago, there was an immigration raid there. The boss said he didn't know he'd hired men sin papeles, but that's bullshit. He knew. A few of them were detained. It's a blessing I got fired.

You nod silently and turn back to the worksheet.

Work hard, mijo, Papi says. Work hard.

I will, you promise.

TURN TO PAGE 000.

The new home you move into sits on a cul-de-sac. It's still in Pomona, and it's not that far from the two-bedroom apartment, but there's more room here. The lawn is yellow, and dirt peeks through the dead grass and stringy weeds. But at least there's a lawn and room to start a garden, one with tomato plants that might rival Abuelita's. She calls weekly, and during the last video call she showed you her garden. It's wilder and more beautiful than ever.

Mami and Papi work year-round, even when you don't have school, so they drop you off at the public library. The summer months are some of the most exciting because the librarians organize special programming to encourage reading. For every book you read, you get a token. If you collect enough tokens, you can exchange them for a free Pizza Hut personal pan pizza.

You spend that summer reading about dragons and Greek mythology. There's air-conditioning in the library, and the librarians don't bother you unless you make too much noise or leave books lying around. Every couple of days a guest speaker comes to the library. Some read you stories, others give educational presentations. One man brings in a bearded dragon, a boa constrictor, and a couple of geckos. Their scales are surprisingly hard and dry against your fingertips.

One of the librarians gives a presentation on the history of Pomona. The first inhabitants of what is now our city were the Tongva, she begins. The city was first settled in the 1830s, while California was still part of Mexico. It was named Pomona after the Roman goddess of fruit, and the rich soil was used to plant citrus orchards. The area was part of the traveling route indigenous people used, and, once it was settled by Mexicans and Anglos from the United States, it continued to be a place where traders and travelers would stop. The city has changed over the years, but it's always been a place for people to call home.

At night, after you've brushed your teeth and slipped into

your pajamas, the places you've called home run through your head. At one point, more than three years ago, your home was made of adobe bricks. It had one window. It felt empty when your parents left, but Abuelita brought you to her home, which she filled with love until it was time to leave. There were other places you called home for a couple of hours, a couple of days. You imagine stepping back through those old, haunted doorways and feeling dirt between your toes or the hot Sonoran sun on your neck.

If you could flip back the pages, you wouldn't. Out of infinite possible homes, you've landed here: a bedroom in Pomona where the air conditioner buzzes softly. A small stack of library books sits atop your dresser. The door is cracked open, and a soft wedge of light illuminates your bedsheets. It might not be the last home you have, but it's an important fork in your journey. Other choices might have led you elsewhere, but no, you are here. Here, Papi pulls a bedsheet over you and pats the edges. Here, Mami gives you a kiss on the cheek good night. Here, you have your parents. You say, I love you, I'll see you tomorrow, and fall asleep knowing they'll be near.

THE END.

TO MOVE ON TO THE NEXT STORY, FLIP
FORWARD TO PAGE 000.

AN
ALTERNATE
HISTORY OF
EL SALVADOR
OR PERHAPS
THE WORLD

For Valeria and Óscar Alberto Martínez Ramírez

THERE IS A RIO GRANDE IN heaven. Óscar and Valeria must cross a million times. It is beautiful, much more beautiful than the river on earth. The water is crystal-clear. The stones in the riverbed shine like amulets. The cattails dance, bending down to touch the warm water, moving side to side so the dragonflies and bluets can zip through. It is so beautiful, and when migrants arrive at the river's edge, they think to themselves: Oh, how muddy and cold, how thundering and tempestuous, how ugly and cruel the other river was. How beautiful this one is.

There is a Rio Grande in heaven. It is so wide, wider than the ocean, wider than a soul. The sky and water are one. The angels are dragonflies and bluets, or cattails dancing on the tiny bit of earth where the migrants stand. Óscar crosses the river many times, but every time, it's effortless. He backstrokes across the warm water. He builds a boat out of mud and buffalo grass and places his daughter against the hull. She laughs fizzy sparks of joy. Óscar and Valeria grow wings, sleek and long like an albatross's, and fly across. All the other migrants follow: in strokes, in boats, with giant wings.

There is a Rio Grande in heaven. It is abstract, too abstract to describe. The water is like spools and spools of cheap tulle. The birds and butterflies are like memories, dreams, desires. The stones dance like drunkards. The current flows like time. It is so abstract, and when the migrants arrive, they don't say anything. Óscar and Valeria stare at their reflections and see the million people they are: dry-cheeked Ophelia, humble Icarus, victorious Captain Ahab, undrowned immigrant. They float on, far above the water, far beyond the river's edge.

There is a Rio Grande in heaven. It is barely a creek. The trickle doesn't sustain much, though loose strands of wild grass poke out from the dry earth. Ladybugs and harvester ants scurry through the dirt, avoiding the migrants' footsteps. Óscar steps over the river, stretching a foot over the soft ripples. It is effortless. His daughter is perched in his arms, and they cross so easily that the river shrivels up. Everyone shuffles over the riverbed. The soles of their feet are dry, and they continue onward to their final destination. The river is an empty wound they leave behind.

ACKNOWLEDGMENTS

If you're the kind of reader who flips to the acknowledgments before you've finished a book: Hello, I see you. Enjoy.

A million little acts of support made this book possible. Naming all of them is impossible, but I'm going to try my best.

Various editors published early versions of these stories over the years, giving me immeasurable confidence in the process: John Joseph Adams at *Lightspeed*, Kolen Kerri at Audible, and Nicole Oquendo at *Aquifer: The Florida Review Online*.

Aemilia Phillips, my fearless agent, always kept the faith. I am endlessly in awe of the good you do, for me and the publishing world at large. The entire SKLA team supported behind the scenes, especially Chandler Wicks and Hannah Schwartz. Tara Taminsky and Shivani Doraiswami at Grandview imagined tremendous possibilities for these stories beyond the page.

Jessica Vestuto, my editor at Mariner Books, understood these stories immediately and cracked them open when I thought there was nothing left to discover. It's a gift to be seen then pushed to be better. Thank you for your guidance and advocacy.

Mariner has been an incredible publishing partner. Special thanks to TK. There is no publishing industry without production teams. I am indebted to mine: TK. María Jesus Contreras illustrated the cover of my dreams.

Brilliant teachers blessed me with the wisdom, rigor, and encouragement that made me a writer. Thank you to every educator who has taught me, especially Glenda Carpio, René

Carrasco, Lorgia Garcia-Peña, and Katerina Gonzalez Seligmann.

The Iowa Writers' Workshop changed my life. Sasha Khmelnik, Deborah West, and Jan Zenisek kept the weird and wonderful place running. I knew so little about writing, but geniuses taught me so much: Alexia Arthurs, Jamel Brinkley, Kevin Brockmeier, Lan Samantha Chang, Abby Geni, and Novuyo Rosa Tshuma. My cohort made attending graduate school at the peak of a pandemic possible and, miraculously, a real delight. Thank you, all.

Over the years, many friends shared places to sleep, meals, drinks, train rides, and their unwavering support. Thank you to Monica Ahrens, Graham Bishai, Tyler Cheng, Natalee Dawson, Dominique Erney, Indya Finch, Joren Francisco, Hannah Friedland, Xochitl Gonzalez, Angela Huang, Kirsten Johnson, hurmat kazmi, Joan Li, William Liauw, Florence Lo, Molly McCabe, Zoë Ortiz, Lukas Ozaeta, Colleen Sam, Santiago Jose Sanchez, Jenika Shastri, Sasha Shpitalnik, Madeleine Taylor-McGrane, Paulina Tiu, Miriam Vélez-Bermúdez, Jen Xu, and many, many others.

For so long, I thought Salvadorans didn't write. Gracias a dios, I was wrong. Javier Zamora, Janel Pineda, and Christopher Soto have inspired me immensely. Gracias, bichxs. It's an honor to be writing alongside you.

I've tried to write about migration as carefully and honestly as I can. Thank you to the family and friends who've shared stories of coming to the United States, including the difficult parts. This work is impossible without you. I'll keep trying my best to get it right.

At various points, the memory of those who are no longer with us guided me forward. Juan Cañadas, Enrique Carpio, Gisella Carpio, Jose Iraheta, Concepcion Reyes, Jose Reyes, Ricardo Reyes, and Adriana Sekiguchi, I carry your presence and love with me every day.

The entire Carpio family helped me build a home in New York. Gisella, I am lucky to be loved by you. Here's to forever.

And finally, my family, who never questioned or ridiculed my dreams of being a writer. What a joy to grow up surrounded by the laughter of so many cousins, aunts, and uncles. Never-ending gratitude to my parents, Ruben and Dolores, and my siblings, Antonio, Rachel, and Kelly. I am always making my way back home to you.

ABOUT
MARINER BOOKS

MARINER BOOKS traces its beginnings to 1832 when William Ticknor cofounded the Old Corner Bookstore in Boston, from which he would run the legendary firm Ticknor and Fields, publisher of Ralph Waldo Emerson, Harriet Beecher Stowe, Nathaniel Hawthorne, and Henry David Thoreau. Following Ticknor's death, Henry Oscar Houghton acquired Ticknor and Fields and, in 1880, formed Houghton Mifflin, which later merged with venerable Harcourt Publishing to form Houghton Mifflin Harcourt. HarperCollins purchased HMH's trade publishing business in 2021 and reestablished their storied lists and editorial team under the name Mariner Books.

Uniting the legacies of Houghton Mifflin, Harcourt Brace, and Ticknor and Fields, Mariner Books continues one of the great traditions in American bookselling. Our imprints have introduced an incomparable roster of enduring classics, including Hawthorne's *The Scarlet Letter*, Thoreau's *Walden*, Willa Cather's *O Pioneers!*, Virginia Woolf's *To the Lighthouse*, W.E.B. Du Bois's *Black Reconstruction*, J.R.R. Tolkien's *The Lord of the Rings*, Carson McCullers's *The Heart Is a Lonely Hunter*, Ann Petry's *The Narrows*, George Orwell's *Animal Farm* and *Nineteen Eighty-Four*, Rachel Carson's *Silent Spring*, Margaret Walker's *Jubilee*, Italo Calvino's *Invisible Cities*, Alice Walker's *The Color Purple*, Margaret Atwood's *The Handmaid's Tale*, Tim O'Brien's *The Things They Carried*, Philip Roth's *The Plot Against America*, Jhumpa Lahiri's *Interpreter of Maladies*, and many others. Today Mariner Books remains proudly committed to the craft of fine publishing established nearly two centuries ago at the Old Corner Bookstore.